HMS SEAWOLF

Other Boson Books by Michael Aye

The Reaper

Barracuda

THE FIGHTING ANTHONYS
BOOK TWO

HMS SEAWOLF

by

Michael Aye

BOSON BOOKS
Raleigh

Michael Aye is a retired Naval Medical Officer. He has long been a student of early American and British Naval history. Since reading his first Alexander Kent novel, Michael Aye has spent many hours reading the great authors of sea fiction, often while being himself "haze gray and underway."

http://michaelaye.com/

Published by
Boson Books, a division of C & M Online Media, Inc.
3905 Meadow Field Lane,
Raleigh, NC 27606-4470
cm@cmonline.com

http://www.bosonbooks.com

ISBN (paper): 1-932482-52-0
ISBN (ebook): 1-932482-53-9

This is a work of fiction and is not an account of actual historical events.

Dedication

To George Jepson who has always had an open ear and good advice.

To James Nelson, a great author who has been more than willing to help a shipmate.

To my grandson, Michael Earl who has made me realize what is truly important in life.

Contents

Acknowledgments viii
Introduction ix

PART ONE 1
The Watch 2
Prologue 3
Chapter One 5
Chapter Two 13
Chapter Three 23
Chapter Four 37
Chapter Five 45
Chapter Six 53
Chapter Seven 65

PART TWO 77
Sailor's Farewell 78
Chapter One 79
Chapter Two 85
Chapter Three 91
Chapter Four 99
Chapter Five 109
Chapter Six 119
Chapter Seven 127
Chapter Eight 135
Chapter Nine 143

PART THREE 161
The Prize 162
Chapter One 163
Chapter Two 177
Chapter Three 195
Chapter Four 219
Chapter Five 229
Epilogue 251
Notes 257
Glossary 259

Acknowledgments

I would like to thank that one special lady who doesn't want her name mentioned, but without her help there wouldn't have been a manuscript. She edits, critiques, and doesn't let me get by with mediocrity.

I want to thank you, the reader, not only for buying *The Reaper* but also for demanding Book Two. I will try to not disappoint you.

A special thanks to Carrie Skalla for her artwork.

Introduction

The early stages of the American Revolution were hamstrung by shortages of gunpowder. At the battle of Bunker Hill the colonists did not have enough to repel the third British charge. A survey by George Washington at the time showed army stockpiles were sufficient for 9 rounds per man.

The British had been careful to restrict the manufacturing of gunpowder in the colonies. British gunpowder was supplied by the Board of Ordnance. The three main magazines were located at Palace Yard, Westminster, the Tower of London, and the largest at Greenwich. From these main magazines, naval supplies were distributed to Ordnance yards close to main dockyards. Overseas bases included Jamaica, Antigua, and Halifax, Nova Scotia.

George Washington's armies totalled about 11,000 men. At the same time there were 11,000 privateers at sea intercepting British shipping in the Atlantic, Caribbean, and even between Ireland and England.

Washington's schooner fleet and privateer raids were directed toward establishing a supply of the precious war commodity as their main objective.

By 1777, the privateers and merchantmen brought in over 2 million pounds of gunpowder and saltpetre.

Privateer John Manley captured the *Nancy*, supplying the American army with 2,000 muskets, 31 tons of musket shot, 7,000 round-shot for cannon, and other ammunition. Captain Jonathan Haraden from Salem, Massachusetts, who captured 1,000 British cannons, was considered one of the best sea fighters, successfully taking on three armed British ships at the same time. Privateers captured countless British reinforcements and over 10,000 seamen, keeping them out of the British Navy.

The capture of the British ship, *Margaretta*, is a true incident. Below is a short description of how the cutter, *Margaretta*, was taken.

> Machias, just east of the Mid-coast region of Maine, was already well populated by June 1775 when a British ship arrived in port accompanied by a cutter, the British warship *Margaretta*. The ships were to return with lumber for the British. The citizens of Machias, who met at a town meeting, declared they would never contribute lumber to the British and erected a liberty pole in the town square to emphasize their declaration. The next day, the Patriots attempted to capture the *Margaretta's* captain, but he stood fast until he was hit by two musket balls. The *Margaretta* surrendered and the captain died. The *Margaretta* was appropriated by the Patriots and was renamed the *Machias Liberty*.

There was a proposal to invade Nova Scotia but not by privateers. It was submitted to General George Washington for action provided there were not more than 200 British troops at Halifax. This can be found on the web at History of Nova Scotia-Communications and Transportation, Chapter 4, 1776, Jan-Dec.

PART ONE

The Watch

The officer of the deck
Peered through the blinding snow
They'd just turned the glass
Only thirty minutes left to go
The distant sound of muskets
A flash as something explodes
Turning to the mid he cussed
Just our luck don't you know

...Michael Aye

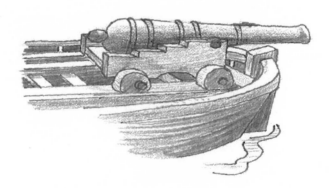

Prologue

BOOM!...KA..BOOM!

"What the hell!"

"I'm not sure, sir, seems like two explosions—a small one, then a larger one."

BOOM!....

"My God, sir, it appears the tender has exploded!"

"Aye, it does," Herrod, the first lieutenant, answered his fifth lieutenant. "Be careful that some of that debris doesn't set Warrior *ablaze, Mr Johns."*

"Aye, sir, I'll call the fire party."

"Mr Dewey."

"Aye," the young mid answered the first lieutenant.

"My compliments to the captain and he may desire to come on deck...Mr Dewey?"

The young mid turned in his stride, "Yes, sir."

"The captain is in conversation with General Clinton and Lord Anthony so be mindful of your manners."

"Aye, sir. Mind them I will."

The harbour was alive with activity. Firelight from at least two blazing ships lit up the snowy night brilliantly when only minutes before a stiff offshore wind had been blowing flurries of snow across the dark anchorage.

"That's musket fire, is it not?"

Turning, Herrod acknowledged his captain. "Aye, sir. Small arm and explosives. What a way to start the first day of 1776, is it not, sir?"

"Aye, Mr Herrod. Happy New Year," Captain Moffett replied dryly.

"Look...Look there, sir," Lieutenant Johns pointed. "Some kind of vessel low in the water next to the transport, Cambridge. It's Cambridge's marines that are firing their muskets at the contraption."

BOOM!...This explosion rocked Warrior and the small group of officers were thrown to the deck. The night sky was even brighter now with large pieces of fiery debris raining down on the ship. As Moffett and his officers regained their feet they could feel the intense heat.

"Mr Herrod!"

"Aye, Captain."

"Beat to quarters if you will, sir. Mr Johns have the fire party form a line with buckets and douse the sails. They're furled and covered with sleet but they could still catch fire with all the debris in the air."

The bosun had to use his starter more than once to move the crew along. Several men appeared frightened and unnerved as they glared at the inferno that was once the proud Cambridge, her bowsprit hanging like a broken tooth. Now her tenders were also ablaze. Other ships had cut their cables to avoid being engulfed in the Cambridge's flames and now several had drifted together, entangling spars and rigging, adding to the mass confusion.

"Quarters, sir. Eleven minutes flat even in this confusion."

"Very well," Moffett answered his first lieutenant. "Now, Mr Herrod, put a couple of boats in the water if you will. I want to be warned if that contraption comes toward Warrior. I'll not have Lord Anthony's flagship destroyed in harbour by some devilish boat only Satan would conjure up."

Chapter One

It was nearing dawn. His Majesty's Brigantine[1] *SeaWolf* was fighting a light wind as she tried to make Barbados before nightfall. Dawkins had laid out his captain's clothes. Today, as everyday when not in port, his boyish captain dressed in sailor's slops. Added always to this were his sea boots and coat. Hot or cold he wore the coat. He might take it off after his first appearance on deck but he always put it on. He rarely wore his hat other than as required by duty.

The captain's hair was jet black with a bit of wave. Well not exactly jet black. The youthful captain had a strip of gray on the right side. A bullet had creased his scalp and when the hair grew back there was a gray furrow. Dawkins watched as his captain stared at his defect. Lady Anthony had said it made young Gabriel more mysterious and romantic to the ladies. Dawkins had not known the captain to lack attention from the ladies, and he had known his young captain several years now. The captain, though only a lieutenant by rank, was a midshipman when they met.

In fact had it not been for the then midshipman Anthony countermanding an order to fire a cannon in gun drill, Dawkins would have lost a leg when the cannon recoiled after being fired. That had created a stir, ending only when Lieutenant Witz had gone mad and jumped overboard. Dawkins had also been present when his captain had made lieutenant. In fact he was an oarsman when "Gabe" had been rowed back to *Drakkar* to inform his brother, Commodore Lord Anthony, he'd passed his exam.

Dawkins was also present that day when *Drakkar* had defeated *Reaper*. He'd been wounded. Nevertheless, when the ketch *Shark* went back to England with Lord and Lieutenant Anthony, Dawkins still recovering from a wound in his arm was made part of *Shark's* crew. Dawkins was no longer fit to be an able seaman. However, he'd learned his numbers and could read and write which was rare for a British tar, and he could perform those duties of captain's steward. He had been pleased by the offer when the captain was given command of *SeaWolf* and gladly accepted. Not because he needed the billet. He'd put up enough prize money to retire, but there was something about his boyish captain that drew Dawkins to him. Something he couldn't explain. He had been to sea more than thirty years and he'd never met another he'd serve this way.

Dagan was talking to the captain. Dagan was a mystery, some said a gypsy soothsayer, but he was the captain's uncle, his protector, and he watched over Gabe like a hawk. Dagan stood watch, and acted as cox'n but otherwise came and went as he pleased, without interference from anyone.

Dagan and Dawkins usually dined together, but Dagan was not much of a talker, therefore Dawkins had learned very little about him beyond what he'd already known from serving with him on *Drakkar*.

The captain was a hard riser. He'd sit on the edge of his chair rubbing his eyes, then run his finger in his hair, take a sip of coffee, then put on a boot. He'd repeat the process for the other boot. Then before putting on his coat, he would clutch the leather bag fastened around his neck. Some wondered what the bag held, but Dawkins knew. It was a large ruby. How it was obtained was questioned in some circles but Dawkins never questioned it. As he touched the bag every dawn the captain would look at Dagan and say "for luck."

***

Lieutenant Gabriel "Gabe" Anthony strode up the companionway to the main deck just before first light. Though the faces were not clearly visible, Gabe knew each of his men. In the few months they'd been together they had meshed into a good crew. A good crew and a good ship.

SeaWolf was a thoroughbred, a brigantine. She was captured at the onset of the war with the colonies. Her master had the ill fortune of being caught on a lee shore by a British frigate and was never able to use the ship for the purpose she was built. She was to have been a predator, a privateer, raiding British commerce. Now she was being used against her former masters.

Gabe, like many, was not sure he agreed with the politics that caused this war with the colonies. He'd do his duty as his brother, Lord Anthony, had often stated, but being a man of intelligence, he had to question some of the British policies. He'd heard Commodore Gardner discuss Lord North's complacency and his underestimation of the colonies' abilities many times.

Well, this ship was proof positive of Britain's complacency about shipbuilding. They'd never have built a vessel like *SeaWolf*. British shipbuilders continued with the same old plans, making the same old mistakes and never seeming to learn. Colonial shipbuilders had recognized the need for change and made modifications to improve a ship's performance. The bow was sharper and cut through the water. The keel was deepened to give the ship more balance under full sail plus the keel was more curved aft so as to draw less water. A brigantine was a swift vessel and more easily manoeuvred than larger ships. It was the perfect privateer.

SeaWolf was one hundred feet long, thirty feet across the beam. She was armed with eighteen six-pounders and six swivel guns. She carried two masts. She was square-rigged on the foremast and on the mainmast, a fore-and-aft mainsail. When needed, staysails could also be bent on.

Gabe's only concern was the gaff and boom. It had caused a few headaches in the early part of the commission but now the crew was wizened to the dangers and no recent injuries had been reported.

Some consideration had been given to the master's comfort when *SeaWolf* had been constructed, leaving Gabe to believe the previous master had likely been a part owner of the vessel if he didn't own it outright. To allow for more head room in the master's quarters a poop deck had been created. The gaff and boom hung amidships over the poop and was manoeuvred by a block-and-tackle that was secured aft to the larboard and starboard sections of the poop. The ship's wheel was located just behind the poop and slightly starboard. *SeaWolf* had been built by shipbuilders who knew their business.

***

SeaWolf's complement was written as one hundred thirty. However, Gabe was happy to have a crew including officers and marines of one hundred twenty-one. Some of the crew had been with Gabe on *Drakkar*. It was a comfort having known men when the commission first began. Everyone now knew their commander's ways; else the bosun would know the reason why.

As Gabe made it on deck he was met by his first lieutenant, Everett Hazard, and the master, Mr Blake. This was Hazard's first commission as an officer. He'd been a pressed man who had flourished in the Navy. He was slightly older than Gabe and would likely end up with a command of his own at some point. He was one of a few who made it to the wardroom from the lower deck. He needed some polish in regards to a gentleman's ways but his seamanship was superb. That was what Gabe needed most, a real seaman.

What could be said about the master? *A breed apart!* He could tell you what the weather was going to do before even the weather knew. He was tall, bald, and leathery. His eyes always seemed to be squinting.

"Morning, Cap'n."

"Mr Hazard, Mr Blake," Gabe answered, a ritual that never changed.

"The wind has started to freshen and a fine drizzle made the dawn seem to linger longer than usual. The hands are at quarters till dawn breaks," Hazard volunteered. "With your permission once we secure from quarters I thought we'd spend some time in sail drill, sir."

"Very well. You're the first lieutenant, Mr Hazard, proceed as you see fit," Gabe answered. It hadn't been that long ago he'd been asking permission before undertaking any task. Gabe wanted Hazard to feel comfortable in his new station. It was not necessary for the first lieutenant to ask permission to carry out duties that were his responsibility and in the months since *SeaWolf* had been commissioned he'd grown with the task. No, Gabe had no complaints.

"Dagan!"

"Aye!"

"Let's go break our fast. It appears Mr Hazard and Mr Blake have everything under control," Gabe said as he headed back to his cabin with Dagan trailing.

By the time Dawkins had poured coffee Hazard was putting the men through their drill.

"Ready ho! Put the helm down."

Gabe could feel the bow begin to swing across the wind.

"Helms a lee, off tacks and sheets."

Yes, Hazard was a seaman. Given time and patience Gabe would have a fine first lieutenant.

Chapter Two

Blasted down by bleak winds, howling at times, heavy rain, then snow and bitter cold, Admiral Lord Anthony and his handful of ships dipped deep into the angry Atlantic swells then fought to rise through the trough, only to dip again, creaking and groaning as living things, heaving through wave after wave.

Lord Anthony shivered as he stood on the quarterdeck of his flagship *Warrior*. He was tempted to go below to his cabin but knew there'd be little relief from the cold other than *Warrior's* wooden walls. In this weather not even the galley fires were lit. As bad as it was on *Warrior*, Anthony knew it had to be worse on the ketch *Pigeon* and cutter *Audacity*. Buck would be better off on *Merlin*, which was a thirty-two-gun frigate. *Damme he hated the cold*, Lord Anthony thought to himself. *How he'd love to be back in the West Indies.*

Thinking of the West Indies, Anthony's thoughts naturally drifted to Gabe. He could see him now, putting *SeaWolf* through her paces. He missed Gabe but knew he had to give him the opportunity to advance. He'd never be able to do that tied to an admiral's coattail.

"Colder'n well digger's arse, ain't it sir?"

"Ah, Bart. I'm surprised you've torn yourself away from Silas's coffee. Did it get cold or did it run out?"

"Well, sir, 'twas a little of both, it be. Silas says if you're to enjoy it afore the heat's all gone to come on down. Otherwise, he'll be taking an ice pick to it."

"Very well, I'll be right down. Bart!"

"Aye, sir."

"My compliments to the captain. Will he take a cup with me if convenient?"

"Aye, sir, I'll see to it," Bart replied as he snuggled his coat tighter about his ears and went to deliver Lord Anthony's message.

"Good morning, Lord Anthony."

"Dutch! Have a seat. Silas has wrapped a hot brick to the coffee pot and is unwrapping it now. He says it's only lukewarm but maybe it'll be stimulating."

"Aye, My Lord, Silas's coffee usually is," Dutch Moffett, Anthony's flag captain, replied, thinking of his first cup of Silas's coffee which had been liberally laced with brandy.

"Looks like the blow will last all the way to Halifax, My Lord. The master says it'll be another two or three days before this lets up."

"Huh," Anthony replied. "I don't know what's worse. Being roasted in New York's harbour or freezing in the Atlantic."

"Well, My Lord, I'm told freezing is less painful."

"Have you ever asked anyone that's been burned alive or frozen to death, Dutch?"

"No, My Lord, I can't say as I have," Dutch answered smiling.

"Then we don't really know, do we?" Lord Anthony quipped. "And I'd rather not learn from experience."

"No, My Lord, neither would I. Speaking of New York, My Lord, they found that contraption that created such a commotion. It's called a submersible or a submarine. One man fits inside and uses a hand crank that turns a propeller that pushes the contraption through the water. A torpedo was attached to a harpoon and driven into the target's hull. Then a fuse is lit. When a signal was given the contraption was hauled away by a party ashore using a tow line attached to its stern. The torpedo fuses were cut at different lengths to give the devil time to do his handiwork before anyone knew something was amiss."

"Not an honourable way to fight a war is it, Dutch?"

"Nay, My Lord, but one has to recognize the genius behind such a scheme."

"Oh, I do recognize that and a lot more as well, especially after my conversation with General Clinton. The Army is treating this war more as an outing than a war. Admiral Shuldham is being sent back to England. Rumour has it Admiral Lord Howe is taking over as Commander-in-Chief, Naval forces.

"I understand Admiral Graves is to be Lord Howe's second and he's to be in charge until Lord Howe arrives."

"Maybe when Lord Howe arrives we will get reinforcements."

"Aye, My Lord, we need them. Twenty-nine ships to patrol eighteen hundred miles of coast from Florida to Nova Scotia. That's a tall order for our entire fleet. It's impossible with our measly twenty-nine ships, most of which are unrated."

"I know, Dutch."

"Bart!"

"Aye, My Lord."

"Have the flag lieutenant bring me those dispatches."

"Right away, sir."

***

"Dreaming of some lass from home are we, sir?"

Lieutenant Francis Markham had been sitting at the wardroom table staring at an empty cup and daydreaming when Bart had stuck his head in the door to deliver His Lordship's summons. The wardroom was generally off limits to the crew, but the officers on board *Warrior* soon learned the Admiral's cox'n pretty much came and went as he pleased.

The fifth lieutenant feeling his prowess in his shiny new uniform had once made the mistake of ordering Bart to report to the bosun for extra duty as he had appeared to have an abundance of time on his hands.

Bart had been sitting aft on the bulwark smoking his pipe. Lord Anthony overhearing the upstart called to his flag captain, "I say, Captain Moffett, would you be so kind as to remind the fifth lieutenant he'd be better suited tending to his duties than interfering in the affairs of my staff?"

"Aye, My Lord. Mr Johns!"

"Yes, Captain."

"Did you hear His Lordship?"

"Aye, Captain."

"Do I have to say more?"

"No, Captain."

"Let's hope not, you damn imbecile. Can't you see his coat's gilded with more gold than you'll ever wear?"

"No, sir, I mean I didn't at the time but I do now, sir."

"Very well then, Mr Johns. Go see the first lieutenant with my compliments and tell him how you're to be available for any additional tasks he might need accomplished."

"Aye, Captain. I'll see him now, sir!"

Since that episode Bart and the rest of Anthony's staff were treated with respect.

***

A loud THUD!

"Zur, the flag lieutenant, zur." The unexpected shout and stamping on the floor made Anthony jump, spilling what was left of his coffee on the flag captain.

"Damme man, I'm not deef."

"Silas!" Lord Anthony exclaimed, then turning to the flag captain he apologized, "I'm sorry, Dutch."

"Yes, My Lord."

"See to Captain Moffett's uniform if you will."

"Aye, My Lord. I'll tend to it now."

Turning back Anthony again apologized, "I'm really sorry, Dutch. I told Dunlap to instruct the sentries to simply knock."

Standing behind Anthony, Bart looked sheepishly at Markham. He and Markham had discussed this situation in the past. Bart couldn't help but believe that the sentry stamped his musket butt on the deck just a little harder than necessary just to see the admiral jump. It was a dangerous game if he and Markham's suspicions were true. Maybe he'd pay the lout a special visit and give a word of warning "Bart style."

"Iffen yews like sir, I's could see the surgeon and get a bit of cotton wadding to stuff in yew's ears so's the sentry wouldn't startle yew so."

"Shut up, Bart."

"Aye, sir. Course we could always flog the bloody bullock so as to make 'em a zample to the utter sentries."

"Bart!"

"Aye, sir. Shut me trap I will and head topside me thinks. It's a little to warm for me liken down here."

As Bart closed the door behind him, Markham exploded with laughter then saw the stare he got from Captain Moffett and Lord Anthony. However, their stare only lasted a moment before they too joined in, causing Markham to start up again.

As always Bart had got the last word in before leaving.

"It's a wonder you haven't set that one adrift," Dutch said when he could catch his breath.

"Aye," Anthony replied, "but Bart grows on you, Dutch. It'd be hard for me to imagine life in the Navy without him."

Markham felt humbled and touched at His Lordship's words.

Sitting in the pantry, Silas shook his head as he was deep in thought. Bart was full of more shit than a holiday turkey. He'd better be glad he was the cox'n. Otherwise, he'd been in a prison hulk somewhere. Some wondered at the relationship between Bart and Lord Anthony. Yes, some wondered but Silas knew.

When His Lordship was a lieutenant and Bart was a seaman on board the brig, *Southwind*, Anthony had caught Flagge, the first lieutenant, sodomizing one of the servants. The captain was not on board and Anthony was unsure of what actions to take. He knew the lout should stand a court martial for buggery. He went ashore that evening and Flagge had Anthony ambushed in an alleyway. Bart had been ashore and happened on the event. While some would have run away, Bart didn't. He'd liked the young lieutenant who was in charge of his division and he hated Flagge. He'd had his own suspicions about the first lieutenant's ways. Bart pulled his knife and picked up a broken barrel stave, and charged into the melee. Bart's intervention saved young Lieutenant Anthony's life. Two of Flagge's men were killed, and two ran off. Bart was shot in the shoulder and Flagge was killed from a knife wound…Bart's knife! After hearing of Flagge's death, the servant fled, never to be heard from again. With both parties gone it would have been difficult to prove Flagge had Anthony attacked.

Although Bart was wounded, it was his glib tongue that made up the story as to how he, Lieutenant Anthony, and the first lieutenant were set upon by thieves. The story was never questioned and Bart had been with Anthony ever since.

***

"Damme, My Lord, but that's a tall order," Dutch had just read the orders that were to employ Lord Anthony's squadron until...

Ye are directed to immediately proceed on a cruize to provide protection of trade for his Majesty's loyal merchants.

Ye are directed to range the coast of Provence of Main...and from thence proceed farr southward as latitude thirty-four north and not further west than the shoals of Nantuckett nor further east than the Island [of] Sable, on the coast of Nova Scotia.

Ye are to remain on station until weather and halidays cease the merchant trade. [2]

After Captain Moffett read Lord Anthony's orders they were returned to Lieutenant Markham to be put away. Markham had read the orders and couldn't help but wonder who had written them. He was not at the top of his class in composition and spelling but he was sure he could have done a better job. This had probably been done by some flag lieutenant who held his commission out of favouritism.

Markham had accepted his present appointment as Lord Anthony's flag lieutenant out of respect. He had the education which some apparently lacked, if those orders were an indication. He had the background and certainly he had the family and Navy name recognition. He had been a midshipman under then Captain Anthony on *HMS Drakkar*. He had made lieutenant at the same time as Gabe, Lord Anthony's brother. He was honoured to be the flag lieutenant and didn't want to appear ungrateful, but what he really wanted was a ship.

Damn Gabe, the lucky sod. SeaWolf. *Now that was as fine a vessel as anyone could hope for as a first command.* He didn't begrudge Gabe his ship; he just wished he could be as lucky. However, he was in the best spot, right here in front of the Admiral should a vacancy arise, or a prize become available. *Damn Gabe, though.* Then Markham felt a bit of guilt at his feeling. He sure missed Gabe, but damn him anyway. He'd buy the first round next time, just because he was such a lucky sod.

Chapter Three

As Gabe strode forward, the wind picked up. He could feel his loose clothing pressed tight against his body and his hair was blowing with the wind. He held onto a shroud as *SeaWolf's* sharp bow cut through the water. He was exhilarated. Fourteen knots, my God what speed, muttered Gabe. He was sure he could coax another knot out of her.

When he was away from the squadron Gabe would put on every inch of *SeaWolf's* canvas and let her fly as he was doing now. Not unlike a thoroughbred at the downs he thought. But Lord Sandwich was right. She was a predator too, and he wondered how long it would be before she fired her guns in anger.

Delivering dispatches was not the type of work Gabe would have chosen but it did allow a certain degree of freedom. One appealing aspect was that it got him away from the squadron and the admiral. An admiral was always an admiral even if he was your brother. He did miss Gil. They had shared some good times and bad ones over the last few years. Gabe had joined his brother's ship as a midshipman but had matured into a man amidst the din of battle.

***

"Sail ho! Two sails on the far horizon!"

"Are they British?"

Gabe turned finding Mr Davy before him—another boy who'd grown into a mature seasoned fighter on board *Drakkar*.

"Why don't you grab a glass and go aloft so that I may have a proper report, Mr Davy?"

"Aye, sir."

"Mr Hazard! Mr Lavery! We might be in for a bit of excitement today."

"Aye, sir," they said in unison, both excited at the possibility of prize money, but Hazard more so than Lavery. Hazard's father had worked at the Boston Company and had been able to help his son advance to master's mate. However, since the war had broken out, Hazard's father had been let go from the firm for not showing enough patriotic enthusiasm. In truth, he agreed with the colonies but felt diplomacy was better than war. Now the family was dependent on Lieutenant Everette Hazard for survival.

Hazard didn't need to be told how lucky he was to have his commission. He felt luckier still having Lieutenant Gabe Anthony as the *SeaWolf's* captain. He'd heard some of the crew tell stories of their captain. It was said he made a fortune in prize money just before the war. Perhaps Everette Hazard might be able to pick up a guinea or two. Watching Mr Davy slide down the shrouds reminded Hazard of what he'd been told of the diminutive young gentleman. Slight in frame he may be, but fearless. Those words from Dagan who rarely spoke. Hazard had seen the long wide scar along Davy's rib cage where he'd been pierced by a huge splinter when *Drakkar* defeated the fifty-gun pirate vessel, *Reaper*. The boy was somewhat of a hero to the men and would make a fine officer. Hazard only hoped he would fair as well, and felt a jealous pang as he thought of the relationship between Davy and the captain. Hazard had also not failed to notice that whenever someone seemed to question Davy's authority, the mysterious Dagan loomed.

"Two sails, Cap'n, just as the lookout said. They appear to be on a nor-nor-westerly heading. However a silvery brown patch off starboard appears to be another set of sails. We should have a better view soon. It's right where blue meets blue and I almost missed it."

Gabe turned to Dagan, "Hear that? He almost missed it."

"Damme sir, but damme the boy's got eyes, ain't he?" Dagan proclaimed.

"Mr Blake!"

"Aye, Cap'n."

"Set us a course to intercept Mr Davy's sighting yonder. Mr Hazard, once we can better identify those sails, be prepared to go to quarters."

"Aye, Cap'n. Think she's a privateer?"

"Who knows, Mr Hazard? My question is why those other two ships left her. They had to have seen her and we've not seen or heard any gunfire. If she's British we'll get the latest news. If she's a privateer we'll fatten our purses."

"Aye, sir. Mine could stand a little fat. It's been lean for a spell now."

"Deck there," the lookout called down. "She's changing her tack."

Gabe looked to his first lieutenant. "No gossip today, Mr Hazard. Beat to quarters if you will, but to be on the safe side put up our signal and see if she answers with the correct recognition."

"Aye, sir."

"Would you like for me to go aloft again, Mr Hazard?"

"Eager today are we, Mr Davy?"

"Aye, sir."

"Mr Davy?"

"Aye, Cap'n."

"I surely expected you to be at your battle station by now and not trying to trick the first lieutenant into approving a skylarking trip for you. Surely, sir, I've not misplaced my trust in you have I?"

"Nay, Cap'n, I'll make you proud," Davy replied as he scampered off to his station, smiling as he noticed Dagan's wink when he passed by him.

"Mr Druett."

"Aye, Cap'n," the gunner answered.

"As soon as we're in range I want you to put a ball across that one's bow."

"Aye, Cap'n, I'll scorch its bowsprit, I will."

"Deck there," the lookout called down, "She be a schooner, sir. Colonial from the looks of things."

BOOM!...Druett had let loose with the forward six-pounder.

"Deck there," the lookout called again, "She's a Jonathan, sir, and she's raised her colours and opened her starboard gun ports. She be a fourteen gunner, sir."

"Very well. Mr Hazard, I want to keep a crew on the forward gun but it's the starboard guns I want manned."

"Mr Blake," Gabe called to the master, "ease her a bit, but be ready to put her helm down. I want to cross her stern and come up on her larboard side so be ready."

"Aye, Cap'n," the master nodded, beginning to understand what his master was about.

BOOM!...Druett had let loose with another shot and it landed just ahead of the chase, drenching all those at the forward guns with its spray.

SeaWolf continued to overreach her prey. Her bow sliced the water as a strong wind caught her sails from dead astern and seemed to slingshot her forward, the wind fairly whistling through the shrouds. *SeaWolf* gained on the schooner at an alarming speed. Dagan was suddenly beside Gabe and said, "She's not handled well, is she," referring to the schooner. *SeaWolf* was now almost directly up with her prey. The deck vibrated as Druett let loose another round, this one striking the schooner about level with the foremast.

"Now, Mr Blake," Gabe ordered, trying to shout above the wind. "Put your helm down. Lively now. Hands to sheets. Reduce sail."

SeaWolf heeled sharply as she crossed in the schooner's wake. Blake could just imagine the bowsprit up the schooners gallery.

"Steady," Gabe called, "Hold her."

Hazard and Blake looked at each other. If *SeaWolf* made it, it was a clever manoeuvre. If not, they'd have a new cap'n very soon. The admiralty didn't take kindly to new captains ramming their ships bowsprit up another ship's arse-hole.

SeaWolf's rudder bit into water and she began to swing just as Gabe had planned. Crossing the schooner's wake caused *SeaWolf* to suddenly list larboard as her gunwales dipped into the trough. A large wave broke over the bow as they broke through the water. Water sluiced down the length of *SeaWolf's* scuppers and hands had to grab hold of something to keep from falling.

"That's it, ease her up now, ease up, full and by. Open your starboard gun ports."

Damn, thought Hazard. They'd crossed the schooner's stern with no more than a chain's length to spare. Hazard's knuckles had turned white from gripping a stay. Now that the manoeuvre was over he felt dumbfounded and grateful they hadn't capsized. He seemed numb. He'd never seen a ship handled so.

"Think he's crazy, don't you?"

Hazard looked at Nathan Lavery, the second and only other lieutenant on board. Without waiting for Hazard to answer Lavery added, "Better get used to it. He's not squeamish."

The roar of *SeaWolf's* cannons startled Hazard. Still somewhat numb and temporarily in thought of Lavery's words, he was caught unaware when Gabe gave the order to fire. Smoke engulfed the ship momentarily till the wind carried it forward.

Thank God Druett has got his wits about him, Hazard thought, *cause I'm making a poor showing.*

"Fire! That's it, lads, fire! Let them Jonathans feel ole *SeaWolfy's* fangs. That's it, now put your backs into it. Swab out. Swab out you buggers."

BOOM!...BOOM!...BOOM!...

SeaWolf's six pounders roared again—gun drill had paid off. The gun crews were like a well-oiled machine.

"Once more now lads, on the up roll fire!"

"Cease fire, cease firing," Gabe bellowed, countermanding his orders from just a breath before. "Cease firing, they've surrendered."

The schooner had struck. A white flag, a shirt tied by the sleeves to a gaff hook was being waved.

"She never recovered from your ruse, Cap'n," Lavery addressed Gabe. "She was ready starboard, but never got a gun in action to larboard. She never fired a shot."

Gabe looked at Dagan. *He knew*, Gabe thought, recalling Dagan's words, *"she's poorly handled."* Gabe didn't feel as joyous as he had a moment earlier.

"Do we send the boat over sir, or do we close and grapple?" Hazard was asking.

"I'll take a boat with the surgeon, I think, Mr Hazard, and have Mr Davy along with the bosun and a few marines come as well."

"Aye, Cap'n."

"Dagan, let's go see to our prize."

***

SeaWolf's broadside had caused much damage aboard the colonial schooner, *Linda Lee*. Spars were down, cordage and riggings were severed and strewn. Several cannons were upturned. Bodies lay about. However to seasoned veterans like Mr Davy and Graf, the bosun, the casualties seemed remarkably few upon first glance. Gabe, along with Dagan, boarded the beaten ship. A youth met them. He still held the gaff with its improvised flag of truce.

"Where are your officers, sir?" Gabe asked.

"Dead. They were trying to help man the larboard guns when you fired your salvo."

Looking about the deck Gabe could see ten or twelve bodies. Another dozen or so of the crew were milling about.

"Where's the rest of your crew?"

"Cap'n Crawford put most of them on prizes and they sailed on to Cuba."

"Where?" Gabe asked.

Realizing he may have given something away the youth became defiant. "None of your business you British bastard."

Davy took a sudden step forward. "Watch your tongue with my cap'n or you'll answer to me."

"That's enough," Gabe spoke to his loyal midshipman. "I'm sure the young gentleman meant no harm."

At that the youth spat on the deck. Mr Davy lunged for the boy only to be stopped by Dagan, who looked dead in the privateering youth's eyes.

"There will be no more. Do we understand one another?"

The youth looked at the cold black eyes that seemed to penetrate into his soul. He could feel the hand of the man who had spoken on his shoulder and suddenly he knew not to push his luck.

"How old are you, boy?" Gabe was speaking again.

"Fifteen sir. Well almost fifteen."

"What's your name, son?"

"Andrew."

"Caleb, will you take Andrew back with you when you're finished here?"

"It will be my pleasure, Gabe. I'm sure he'd like to meet Mr Jewells."

Mr Jewells was Caleb's ape. Only a few knew his name was a reflection on part of his anatomy and not his disposition.

"Dagan, let's have a look at the captain's cabin. Mr Graf, send a party through the ship checking for damage and anything that may be of interest. Lieutenant Baugen, put a sentry on the rum stores. I'm sure there's some about, then have the prisoners searched for weapons, then get them in the hole."

"Aye, Cap'n, we'll take care of it," Baugen replied. Then turning to his men, "Marines, do your duty as the cap'n has ordered."

"Mr Davy?"

"Yes sir, Cap'n."

"Signal for Mr Hazard to join me on the prize."

"Aye, aye sir."

***

"Sail ho! Fine on the larboard bow," the lookout called down his sighting.

Lavery approached the master and Dagan.

"Two in one day?" The master raised his thick bushy eyebrows, "If the Lord giveth, who are we to question his bounty?"

"Deck there, she's the *Badger*, sir. I've seen her in Barbados afore."

"Francis Fewghay of His Majesty's armed brig, *Badger*," the captain introduced himself to Gabe as he came aboard *SeaWolf*. "I'm part of Vice Admiral Gayton's squadron. I'm on the way to Barbados by way of Port Royal, Jamaica.

As Dawkins served the officers a glass of wine, Fewghay asked, "Have you heard Admiral Lord Howe is now in command of the North American Naval Forces. Admiral Shuldham has returned to England."

"What about Admiral Graves?" Gabe asked.

"He's going back as well, but word is he'll return after refit and overhaul."

Touching Gabe's arm Fewghay almost whispered, "Rumour is Admiral Gayton is not well and will likely be returning to England soon also." Gabe wondered if Gayton was ill or just didn't look forward to the trying times ahead.

***

"Land ho," the lookout called halfway through the forenoon watch.

"Where away," Hazard called, his impatience at not already having been told not lost on the lookout.

"Two points off the starboard bow," came the answer.

Hazard went aloft with his telescope to identify the land. The eastern point of the island was visible. Quickly sliding down the stays Hazard quipped, "A perfect landfall."

"What else should we expect from our master?" Gabe joined in.

"We'll be entering Carlisle Bay soon," the master advised, feeling somewhat smug and strutting like a peacock.

"Let's make the ship ready to enter port," Gabe instructed his first lieutenant. He'd not have the admiral mentioning any defects if he could help it.

"Aye, sir, she's looking smart now but we'll smarten her up another notch."

Gabe then motioned to Dagan to follow as he went below to put together *SeaWolf's* papers for the admiral along with usual dispatches and his reports on the capture of the prize. *SeaWolf* and her prize sailed to Barbados in company with *Badger.*

They rounded Needham Point and then tacked into Carlisle Bay. The master checked the bay depth for the anchor, and the gunner was making ready for the salute. No sooner had the salute been given than the flagship signalled "Captain repair on board." Dagan had the gig ready and as they rowed over to the flagship, Gabe marvelled at the light green colour of the water inside the bay. It was here he had met Caleb. Would he remember that night? With the antics of Caleb's ape, he thought how could he forget.

"Flagship, sir."

Damn, Gabe thought, *I've been daydreaming.*

Admiral Gayton handed the dispatches to his flag lieutenant to sort while a servant fetched Gabe a glass of refreshing lime juice. The heat in the admiral's cabin reminded Gabe of just how cold it had been when he'd left New York. You couldn't find a warm spot. After reading Gabe's report on capturing the *Linda Lee* the admiral spoke.

"Not much fight in the Jonathans would you say, sir?"

A little surprised at the admiral's tone, Gabe swallowed his lime juice before answering, "There wasn't that many on board to put up much of a fight, sir. Her captain had dangerously under-manned her, providing prize crews for the ships he'd taken."

Gabe was again surprised when the admiral's tone changed, "It does you credit, sir, to be so honest. I know those who would have doubled the number of enemy dead to make them look better."

Gabe breathed a little easier. He'd passed the admiral's little test.

"Did the boy say where they were home ported?"

"Not to me, sir," Gabe answered the admiral, "But when talking to my midshipman he stated that Port Royal, South Carolina was home. That's just down the coast from Charlestown."

"Hmmm," was the admiral's only reply as he scanned the pages Gabe had obtained from the captain's cabin of the prize. "That damnable fellow Crawford knew his business," the admiral continued. "He's captured a transport from Antigua laden with gunpowder on her way to Halifax. No wonder he's undermanned the schooner. The transport was worth her weight in gold. He's also taken a merchantman loaded with winter uniforms, rifles for sharpshooters, and ammunition. He's also captured three colliers loaded with coal but he doesn't say where. A busy man is he not?"

"Aye," Gabe replied.

Dropping the inventory sheets to his desk the admiral rubbed his brow and his face seemed to sag. The news of the captures by the privateer Crawford seemed to burden the admiral.

"You know," the admiral said addressing Gabe once again, "We just lost a brig loaded with three hundred and eighty-six barrels of gunpowder as she was headed to Philadelphia. Do you know what that does to our abilities to fight and sustain an engagement sir?"

The admiral continued on without giving Gabe the opportunity to reply. "America does not have the ability to produce large quantities of gunpowder. In England, gunpowder is distributed to the ordnance yards at Chatham, Portsmouth, and Plymouth. It is from there it's then transported to Gibraltar, Jamaica, Antigua and then on to Halifax, Nova Scotia. From there it's distributed to where it's needed. At this point in the war, British forces are hamstrung by shortages of gunpowder."

Standing and walking to the stern gallery Gayton said, "I'm sending you to Antigua. A convoy is soon to leave there for Halifax. Can you guess what the cargo is? Yes, I'm sure you can."

Again, the admiral didn't allow Gabe to respond. "I know you would rather do something more exciting than escort a bunch of slow merchantmen but that gunpowder has to reach Halifax. Do I make myself clear?"

"Yes, sir," Gabe answered.

As if on cue there was a knock on the door. The flag lieutenant entered. "I have everything ready, sir."

Gabe knew the interview was over. As he made ready to depart the admiral addressed him once more.

"I'll buy the schooner into the service. Do you have anyone senior enough to command her?"

Taken aback and overwhelmed by the admiral's offer Gabe could only mutter, "Not here sir," but his thoughts were on Francis Markham. He'd love her.

As Gabe made his way out the admiral called, "Give my regards to your brother and congratulate him on his flag."

"Aye, sir, I will."

"Gabe?"

"Sir," Gabe was surprised at being addressed so.

"My condolences in regards to the loss of your father. He was a fine officer and would be proud of you. If ever I can be of any service you have but to contact me."

Finally, leaving the admiral's stateroom, Gabe could only shake his head. *Damned if he ain't human!*

Chapter Four

Entering English Harbour brought back bittersweet memories for Gabe. He thought of the lavish parties he'd attended when *Drakkar* had used the island as her base for operations against the pirates. He also recalled his bout with near death after one encounter with the rogues. However, his youth didn't let his mind dwell on the dreary. The island women! That's where his thoughts travelled and lingered. The island women ranged from tavern doxies ready to pleasure the jack tars, to well-kept mulattos who could turn a man's head in a second. Many a duel had been fought over these half-white, half-black women. There were also the rich, ripe young planter's daughters. They were usually looking not only for a husband but a way off the island. And then there were the island widows. Some of them so rich a Spanish galleon couldn't carry their gold. They used men as playthings, to satisfy their needs but rarely anything else.

Gabe recalled Lieutenant, now Captain Buck, having an on and off affair with such a lady. "It's lasted because we're at sea so much," he had volunteered one night on watch. "I'm gone before she gets bored, but I'll not complain. Nay, no complaints on my part."

***

Dagan and Dawkins had come ashore with Gabe while the purser and a working party had been sent to find fresh fruit and vegetables for the crew. A lesson passed down from

Vice Admiral Anthony to his sons. Keeps the scurvy at bay. Both sons had listened well and insisted every effort be made to keep them on board regardless of the purser's protest and complaints about expense. It was a short walk to the government house at the top of the coast road. One Gabe had made many times.

However, this time would be different. Commodore Gardner wouldn't be there to greet him like a friend. Today he'd be just one more junior officer reporting as required. *Damned if it ain't a scorcher today*, Gabe thought. There was the hint of a breeze that made his shirt stick to his body. In the old days he'd have come ashore without his coat but not today. The tease of a breeze was gone. The flag hung limply against the flagstaff. Unlike on previous visits there were only a few workers in the yard surrounding government house. Entering the building brought an immediate relief from the sun's heat. The marine sentry snapped to attention and directed Gabe to his sergeant who directed him to a clerk. The clerk, acting like he was at Whitehall, had him sit in an office till the commodore could be with him. It was a familiar office, Gardner's old office.

Gabe rose and walked to the window. Below at the anchorage Gabe could make out a variety of ships. A sixty-four-gun two-decker was probably the commodore's flagship. He could also see island schooners, small fast ships plying their trade through the Leeward Islands. There was also a group of merchant and supply vessels. Undoubtedly, some of these would be with the convoy he had to herd to Halifax.

Hearing the door open and close, Gabe turned and spoke, "Lieutenant Anthony, sir, in command of *SeaWolf*."

Taking the offered dispatches, the new commodore sat in his chair behind the great desk.

"I ask for convoy protection and what do I get, a wormy brig, a privateer's ship with a junior officer and a schooner that's not got enough firepower to scare a gnat. Frigates, that's what I need."

Unsure of what to say, Gabe said nothing. "When were you commissioned?" the commodore asked.

"January '76," Gabe replied but then added, "from this office."

"What was your last ship?"

"*HMS Drakkar 44*, Commodore Anthony."

"Any kin?"

"My brother."

"Huh! Your father was?"

"Vice Admiral James Anthony."

"I knew him," the commodore replied. "I also know Gardner and he has spoken highly of you, so we'll see if you rate his praise. I've called a meeting of the captains of the ships you are to escort. It will be here in this building at four o'clock. By then your documents will be ready. You are the senior by one month so you will be in command. Lieutenant Bruce commands the brig *Lancaster*. Why I don't know. He wouldn't know what to do with her if someone stuck her up his arse and fired a broadside."

"I'll do my duty, sir."

"No doubt," the commodore replied. The interview was over.

Still feeling the commodore's heat, Gabe felt that the Caribbean sun felt hotter than when he entered the building if that was possible. Dagan was leaning against one of the piles smoking his pipe when Gabe made it to the ship's boat.

"All ready?" Gabe asked.

Taking his pipe from his mouth and exhaling a puff of smoke, Dagan commented, "That bad was it?"

"It was."

"Know who the commodore is?"

"Merriam, Commodore Webster Merriam."

"He's Witzenfeld's uncle on Witz's mother's side."

"How do you know?"

"I went to get a wet and the tavern keeper told me." No wonder he acted so Gabe thought.

***

Returning to the landing, Gabe and Dagan were surprised to find one of their boats still there. On the chance of seeing Commodore Gardner, they had gone up to Lady Deborah's main house. The commodore and his wife were living there since he'd retired.

"There's no sense in the main house sitting empty," Lady Deborah had said when the commodore retired. The merchant owner had found he needed the property the Gardners had been living in. It probably had more to do with the loss of Navy contracts Gardner had been funnelling to him than any need of property.

However, with Lady Deborah in England and Lord Anthony at sea, she had both the main house and the cottage vacant. The cottage would be kept vacant should it be needed by the family if the opportunity to spend time on the island arose. Unfortunately, Gabe and Dagan arrived at the main house only to find the commodore and Greta had gone to St. Johns. The trip had taken over an hour and Gabe had expected to hire a boat or catch a ride back to *SeaWolf*.

"Mr Davy, why ain't you back at the ship?"

"We've been waiting on the purser, sir. Him and the surgeon."

"The surgeon."

"Aye," Davy replied. "He said he wanted to replenish some of his medicines he was low on, sir, but I didn't believe him."

"You didn't, and why pray tell is that, Mr Davy?"

"Cause sir, he took that damn ape along and he don't usually do that if its business."

This response brought guffaws from the crew. Caleb's ape, Mr Jewells, had become something of a celebrity throughout Lord Anthony's command but without His Lordship's endorsement.

Gabe and Dagan looked at each other. Mr Davy was very astute and had a keen sense of observation but neither spoke about it.

"Excuse me, sir," one of the boatmen said. "Me thinks dats the purse-or huffing and puffing his way down de jetty now."

All turned to see the purser hurrying his way along. His cheeks were red and puffing, his breathing laboured and his clothes drenched in sweat. Taking off his hat and wiping his face with a rag he tried to catch his breath so he could talk, then rubbed the same rag through his sparse hair, plastering the few sprigs to his head.

"Damme, Mr Petrie, why such an all fire hurry? You'll likely fry your brain rushing about in this heat with such a burden."

"Sir," Petrie was gasping his breath as he tried to address Gabe. His pot belly and chest were heaving. "It's...the...surgeon...sir. I thought I ought to hurry...he's about to fight a duel..."

"A duel," Gabe exclaimed.

"Aye, sir," Petrie's breathing was coming a bit easier now. "I thought you oughta know quick like."

"Where?" Gabe asked.

"The Sugarcane, sir."

Gabe knew it well. Not a tavern for the common sailor; but neither was it an elite establishment. An out-of-the-way place where deals were made, both financial and sexual.

"Dagan, you come with me. Mr Davy, let Lieutenant Hazard know where we are."

Gabe knew Davy knew the location of the place from experience. His first experience in becoming a man.

"Should we send for Lieutenant Baugean or maybe his sergeant," Petrie asked.

"No," Gabe replied, already headed for the tavern, "Dagan and I will handle this."

***

Caleb McKean was the nephew of Lady Anthony's first husband. He was Gabe's best friend and a physician. He had saved Gabe's life as well as the lives of many during their battle with pirates just before the war with the colonials. He had been the one who removed the huge splinter from Mr Davy's side. Lord Anthony had said, "Caleb is an excellent physician, he's rich on manners, but damn poor on morals."

Lord Anthony had tried to lure him into the Navy but as a physician he would not take a step down for a surgeon's warrant. His being on board *SeaWolf* had caused His Lordship to raise his brow. Gabe had stated the surgeon who had been assigned to *SeaWolf* had somehow been delayed and the ship had had to sail without him.

And wasn't it convenient Caleb just happened to be present to fill the vacancy Lord Anthony had queried.

He knew Gabe's explanation of events wouldn't hold water, but if Caleb was of a mind to serve as a physician for Gabe without pay he wouldn't forbid it as long as he conformed to regulations and didn't interfere with Gabe doing his duty. Lord Anthony also remembered it was Caleb who had saved his brother's life after a fierce and bloody battle.

When Gabe and Dagan entered the tavern Caleb and the ape were drinking ale. Things didn't appear to be as serious as the purser had stated but on a closer look Gabe noted Caleb's brace of pistols lying close at hand, loosely pointed at a man and woman sitting at the closest table.

Both were hovered close together. The woman had more "wares" showing than covered. They both looked like and smelled like they hadn't had a bath in some time.

"How goes things, Caleb?"

Looking up, Caleb smiled. "Just finishing my ale. Would you and Dagan care to join me for another round?"

Mr Jewells, the ape, had turned his tankard upside down and was swiping the inside with a finger then licking his finger. He'd made a face not unlike a smile to show all his teeth. Then he rolled his lips over, straightened his face, and grunted. He tried to steal Caleb's tankard. Caleb popped the ape's hand, but not hard, and said, "No, you've already had two rounds." This caused more grunting that increased in intensity into a screech. Caleb said, "Hush…" The ape would of course pick up his tankard again only to begin the cycle anew.

"The purser thought you might be in a bit of difficulty," Gabe said by way of explaining his and Dagan's presence.

"No difficulty now that yonder lout and his wench and I have come to an understanding."

Looking once more at the two, Dagan whispered to Gabe, "Man's holding a bloody rag to his ear."

To this Caleb said, "That good fellow tried to pimp his wench off on me. I refused. Then he gave a list of particular services she could perform, some of which a gentleman wouldn't repeat. Just for a bottle of rum. I once again declined the foul-breath fool and this time I laid my pistols on the table to emphasize we had no interest."

By "we", Gabe was not sure if Caleb had another with him during the conversation or he meant Mr Jewells and himself.

Caleb continued, "Then the pest had the wench expose herself by hiking her skirt (she wasn't wearing any drawers), and offering herself to Mr Jewells." Caleb then returned to his ale.

"Well, what happened then Caleb?" Gabe demanded.

"Why Mr Jewells picked up one of my pistols and shot the fool's ear off."

"Shot him!"

"Aye, Gabe." Then Caleb seemed very serious, even though his words were slurred from too much drink. "Gabe, you outta know there's some things even an ape won't do."

Chapter Five

Coffee, sir," Dawkins stood by the table where Gabe sat, "Sip careful, sir, it's still 'ot." Dawkins had been told of the events at the tavern by Dagan as the two had smoked their pipes last evening. The mental picture kept coming to the old man's mind and he found himself chuckling at the thought of the ape shooting off the man's ear. *Was it purely an accident? What would have happened if the shot was a bit further over?*

As Gabe sipped the coffee he felt his stomach growling. For some unexplained reason he felt apprehensive about this convoy. It was up to him to herd the ordnance transport filled with gunpowder along with three other supply ships so overloaded they appeared to be bulging. There were also a couple of troop ships. One was for the southern campaign at Charlestown and the other for New York. They would move at a snail's pace. Two thousand miles or so at the speed of the slowest sailor. Then up to New York and finally Halifax. They'd be lucky not to run out of rations before they got to Charlestown.

The commodore was right. The brig, *Lancaster,* looked as if she might sink at any moment. Years in the tropics would do that to a ship, especially one that hadn't been coppered. Gabe believed her wizened old master when he said, "She needs scraping but otherwise she's sound." Gabe found Lieutenant Bruce to be as the commodore described. I'd not put him in charge of a bumboat much less a brig, Gabe thought. He was doubly glad of her master.

Lieutenant Estes, captain of the *Wild Goose* seemed very capable. It was almost shameful, the relief on Bruce's face when he found out not only would Gabe be in command but also Lieutenant Estes would be his second if anything should happen.

The *Wild Goose* looked fairly new. She was an American made schooner and would handle well, Gabe knew from previous experience. However, she was less than eighty feet long, had a crew of seventy to seventy-five and carried only ten six-pounders and a few swivels for armament.

Again, as the commodore had said, not much firepower to protect the convoy they were to escort. Dagan came in as Gabe was finishing his coffee.

"Mr Hazard said the wind has freshened. Some of the convoy has already gotten underway without your signal."

Damn, Gabe thought, recalling the words from the *Turtle's* captain. "We know when and how to sail, Navy boy, you just protect us." *So much for meetings.* Hazard met Gabe as he came on deck.

"Anchors hove short."

"Very well, up anchor, Mr Hazard, loosen the head sails. Make general signal to get underway."

No sooner had the signal been given when Lavery reported, "*Wild Goose* has already gotten the wind in her sails.

"Main the braces" Gabe eyed *Wild Goose*. He didn't want it to appear a race but he didn't like being beat. Not when it was suppose to be him calling the shots.

"Sir," Hazard called, "I don't see any action on board the *Lancaster*."

"Mr Davy!"

"Aye, sir."

"Signal *Lancaster*. Make haste!" Hands aloft, Mr Hazard. Loosen the fore topsail."

SeaWolf had made her way through the winding array of ships in the anchorage.

"Winds appears to be picking up, sir," the master volunteered. "Should make for fine sailing."

"Mr Davy!"

"Aye, sir."

"Make general signal to convoy to form line behind *SeaWolf*. Signal *Wild Goose* to take station to leeward and *Lancaster* to windward."

"Aye, sir."

Halfway through the first watch Gabe made it down to his cabin, so tired he collapsed into his chair. He now saw his brother and father in a new light. Holding command was not always all claret and prize money, as someone had once put it. Keeping the convoy together took more coaxing and bullying than Gabe would have imagined. He was physically and mentally drained. He'd had to have *Wild Goose* surge ahead and put one across *Turtle's* bow to make her comply with sailing orders.

Turtle's master had closed to hailing distance with *SeaWolf* before taking her position in the convoy. Captain Patrick in his brogue Irish had threatened Gabe for his high-handedness and promised Gabe he'd hear from high authority.

"He's just trying you," Dagan had said.

Thankfully, *Lancaster* had remained on station and responded when Gabe had signalled changes. "Her master's a good man," Blake reassured Gabe. "We were mates together on the old *Ogdon*. He knows what he's about. He'll keep station."

To which, in one of his rare demonstrations of temper, Dagan had responded, "Hell, a man with a good set of oars in a row boat could keep station with us."

Maybe that was it, Gabe thought. They were used to independence and flying with the wind. Not creeping along at five knots.

***

It seemed like an age since they'd set sail from English Harbour, but after that first day everyone had settled down to routine. They'd shortened sail at night and carried all the canvas the ships could handle during the day. All sorts of drill had been practiced and competitions had been set up to keep the crew busy so they wouldn't get sullen. Only one man had been flogged.

However, if the master was right they should sight land the next afternoon; if not, then early the following day. Some of the weariness he'd felt that first day still lingered, but overall he was much better. Dawkins was there as always with that much needed first cup of coffee. It had been hard to get to sleep the previous evening and harder still getting up. Gabe would never be an early riser.

The early gray light of dawn was starting to penetrate the stern windows. The lanthorn was still needed but not for long. Looking up at the lanthorn he noticed it swinging more than usual. Then Gabe realized there was more than the usual roll as *SeaWolf* made her way. When Dagan entered the cabin moments later he found Gabe almost completely dressed.

"You feel the wind?" he asked.

Gabe nodded his answer as he took a sip of Dawkins's fresh hot coffee. Once on deck Gabe found the master and first lieutenant together.

"Morning, sir." Lavery had the watch. "Looks like we're in for a blow. I hope we don't lose any of our cows." Lavery took particular delight into referring to the merchantmen thusly.

"We're in for a gale, sure enough," the master confirmed. "Not unusual when the warm Caribbean waters and the cold Atlantic waters come together at this time of year. We're in for rain and maybe some hail. The wind is from the east heading west-nor-west. I'd keep the sails reduced, sir, or we may find ourselves on a lee shore before we know it."

The rains came quickly and in sheets; then with the wind picking up the temperature dropped, and then the rain became sleet. Desiring to look at the compass, Gabe and the master half-walked and half-slid across the deck to the binnacle.

"Damned if I ain't half-blinded," the master complained. Gabe had Hazard change the men on deck every half-hour. With no fire it wasn't much better below deck but at least the crew was out of the wind and rain.

"No cause to be anxious yet, Cap'n, but it wouldn't hurt my feelings none if we was to change our course a point or two to the north."

"I was thinking the same thing," Gabe replied, "But we can barely see the next ship in line and I'm sure their captain would never see a change of course signal."

"Maybe we could fire a gun, sir," Lavery volunteered.

"Think they'd hear it in this wind?" Gabe said. "No, we'll stay on course, but if by the first dogwatch the weather hasn't moderated we'll have to do something."

"Aye, Cap'n," the master answered as he wiped sleet from his face. "I think I'll take another look at my charts."

***

The sleet did stop and the wind died down to a moderate breeze. "Not a moment to soon for my liking," Blake declared. "Another hour and I doubt we could've beaten our way off a lee shore."

Gabe looked at the master. His kind always seemed to be overly cautious, but a prudent captain always listened to his master. Lieutenant Hazard had the glass to his eye. "I see *Wild Goose* and two of the convoy but the rest are no where to be seen, including the *Turtle* and the *Lancaster*.

"Should we send up a flare, sir?" This from Lieutenant Lavery. "Maybe they'll see that." A flare every ten minutes had been agreed upon for situations like this, but Gabe was hesitant.

"Mr Davy."

"Aye, Cap'n."

"Go aloft with a glass and see what you can, including land. We have a few minutes of daylight left so perhaps you'll spot something."

Without speaking, Gabe looked at Dagan who nodded, "I'll go skylarking with you, Mr Davy, but mind you, I'm too old to go racing through the ratlines like Caleb's ape." This brought a smile to the little group.

Gabe's father, Vice Admiral Anthony, had always said, "Dagan's got the best peepers I ever did see." Well, hopefully he could pick up something now.

When the two got back on deck, Dagan let Mr Davy make his report. "Two sails dead astern, sir, and I think the brig is abeam on the weather side. That's in addition to *Wild Goose* and the troop ships we can see from deck."

"So one of our eggs is missing, a turtle egg. I shouldn't wonder," Gabe said aloud, and then asked, "What about land?"

Mr Davy looked to Dagan who answered, "Nothing for sure but by the way the clouds appear I'd say we're close. I also think *Turtle* is dead ahead by ten miles or so."

Gabe had the feeling that there was more but didn't push it. "Better send up flares, Mr Hazard."

"Aye, Cap'n."

Turning to speak to Dagan, Gabe's eyes seemed to blur and he suddenly felt dizzy and nauseated. "I think I need to go below," he said suddenly, and as he turned, collided with the bosun.

"My gawd, sir," Graf said, "You're burning up."

Dagan helped Gabe to his cabin and sent Mr Davy for Caleb. After speaking with Gabe, Caleb said,

"You've developed the humours, sir. A malodorous humour more than likely due to the stress one has placed on his system without allowing time for the habitus to rejuvenate. I do hope this malady is not due to a contagion. Now Dawkins will give you a tea made of willow bark to help with agues. I've added lemon and honey so that the tea will be more palatable. A generous dollop of brandy may also help you rest better. Now sir, I shall require you retire to your bed and not be disturbed until the morrow."

With a word to Dawkins to send for him should any further symptoms arise Caleb headed for the wardroom. When Caleb had left, Dagan came over and sat by Gabe's cot.

"What else did you see," Gabe asked.

"Maybe nothing but maybe three sails, just on the horizon. Fine on the starboard bow."

"Which direction was they headed?"

"The light was too bad to tell," Dagan replied, "But tomorrow we'll know."

Dagan helped Dawkins get Gabe's boots off so he could rest properly. Then Dagan helped Gabe sit up while Dawkins administered Caleb's concoction.

"Damn," Gabe grimaced. "I thought the lemon and honey was to make the tea palatable."

"More palatable was Caleb's exact words, I believe," Dagan smiled. "You know Caleb, cure ye or kill ye, makes no difference. Either way, you quit complaining.

Chapter Six

C ap'n...Cap'n..." Dawkins was speaking, and slowly the fog cleared from Gabe's head.

"I'm awake," he said, "What time is it?"

"First light, Cap'n. I let you rest a bit longer. How do you feel this morning?"

"Right now I feel fine," Gabe answered the old sailor as he rose from his cot.

"I got your coffee ready, sir. Do you want it afore or atter your tea?"

"My tea?"

"Yes sir," Dawkins replied. "The doctor said to give it to you right off. I've got it ready."

Just thinking of the concoction made Gabe's body give an involuntary shudder. "Well, let's be done with the damn stuff, then maybe I can enjoy my coffee. Where's Dagan?"

"He went topside to have a stretch. He spent the night in yonder chair."

"He stayed here all night long?"

"Aye, Cap'n."

"There was no need of that. He should have rested in his own hammock."

"Begging the Cap'n's pardon, but who was gonna tell him to leave? Not me or anyone else what's got a brain."

A knock at the door and the sentry announced, "Mr Davy, sir."

"Come in, Mr Davy. How are we this fine Navy day?"

"I'm well, Cap'n. How are you this morning? You put a scare in us last evening."

'I'm fine, sir, but is that why you're here, to inquire as to my health?" Gabe asked.

"Oh no, sir, the first lieutenant's respects, sir, but are you coming on deck or should he present himself to your cabin, sir."

This caused Gabe to stop. "Is there an emergency, Mr Davy?"

"Nay, sir, but I believe they've sighted land and several sails. Dagan has gone aloft."

"Very well, Mr Davy. Tell the first lieutenant I'll be topside directly."

"Aye, sir."

Once on deck, Gabe found both Lieutenant Hazard, Lieutenant Lavery, and the master amidships. Mr Hazard held a glass to his eye. The master was first to spot him.

"Morning, Cap'n."

"Mr Blake, Mr Hazard, Mr Lavery," Gabe addressed each, as was his morning ritual.

"The lookout has spotted land, sir. It appears we're a little off course," Hazard reported.

Hearing this Gabe turned to the master. "Mr Blake, what's your calculation?"

"We've been pushed south by the gale, sir. I believe we are just off the coast of South Carolina but instead of Charlestown sir, I think we are about sixty miles south, possibly Port Royal or one of the barrier islands. There are several of them."

Dagan had made his way down from the masthead. "There are three strange sails, two appear to be schooners and the other larger. About the size of a brig. *Turtle's* still about ten miles ahead and from the looks of things I'd say they've spotted her."

"Privateers you think?" Hazard asked.

"That'd be my guess," Gabe answered.

"But I thought they'd be bottled up by our blockade and lazing by the fire," Lavery commented.

"I'm sure they used the gale as a means of running the blockade," Gabe answered. "I'm not sure I'd risk broaching my ship in such a gale just to run down a bunch of privateers I probably couldn't catch and that'd likely end up on a lee shore anyway."

Then Gabe asked, "What about the rest of the convoy?"

"They're on station sir, including *Wild Goose* and *Lancaster*. I fired the flares as you ordered before you took ill," Hazard continued, "but *Turtle* never responded."

"I didn't expect her captain would," Gabe answered. "The arrogant son of a bitch is probably going to cost us a lot before this day's over, gentlemen, especially with those privateers lurking. Did you log his failure to respond, Mr Hazard?"

"Aye, Cap'n, last night and this morning."

"Very well, the wind is almost directly astern so have Mr Druett fire one of the forward guns. He's bound to hear it. I know he's not deaf."

"Think we should signal for him to take up station, sir?"

"It wouldn't hurt. However, he didn't answer the flares so I doubt he'll answer the signal."

Feeling his stomach growl, Gabe realized he hadn't eaten in twenty-four hours. "Dagan, let's go below. Mr Hazard let me know if there's any change."

Once below, Dagan spoke, "You think he's ignoring the signals on purpose, don't you?"

"Yes," Gabe answered, "I think he's got a rendezvous set up with the privateers. Why else would a man be in such a hurry to risk himself and a load of gunpowder."

***

After a fitting breakfast and two cups of coffee Gabe returned back on deck. Lieutenant Hazard reported, "I was just about to send for you, sir. The *Turtle* has taken a more southerly course and the privateers seem to be ignoring her and headed toward us."

Gabe pounded the bulwark with his fist, 'I knew it." Then he explained his theory to his first lieutenant. "Signal *Lancaster* to come abeam on the weather side. Then have Estes to position *Wild Goose* behind *Lancaster* about midway through the convoy. If one of the privateers get through it's up to him to protect the convoy."

"Deck there," the lookout called down, "The ships be separating, sir. One's ship rigged, sir, she be about eight miles off the starboard bow. The schooners, sir, one going to windward and tother to leeward."

"Separating to get amongst the convoy," the master said while holding a ship's glass to his eye. "I can see the t'gallants of one."

"Signal *Wild Goose* to be ready, Mr Hazard, but tell him to stay on station for now. Let's see what their next move is."

"Aye, Cap'n."

"Damn, sir," the master called, "That un looks like she might be a French corvette."

"I'll go aloft," Dagan volunteered.

"Beat to quarters, Mr Hazard."

"Aye, Cap'n."

Dagan was down on the deck before Gabe realized it. "She's a corvette right enough and appears to be a twenty-four."

"Damme," Gabe exclaimed. "I bet she's got a crew of a hundred and fifty or more." Sensing there was more, Gabe stopped talking and looked at Dagan. "What else?"

"She's flying the same company flag as that prize we took on the way to Barbados."

"So they're after blood as well as the convoy," Gabe muttered to himself.

"The wolves will be in firing distance in ten minutes or so, Cap'n," Mr Hazard said, "She's under full sail."

"In a hurry that one, ain't she," the master said.

"Deck there…The schooner to leeward has dropped back and appears to be taking the weather gage."

"I didn't think she'd keep her previous station," Gabe stated, "That was just a ploy to see how we responded."

"Deck there," the lookout howled down, "She's run out her larboard guns!"

"Deck there," the lookout called again, "The furthest schooner, she be sailing wide and putting on more sail."

"A wolf trying to get among the cows."

"Sheep, Mr Lavery, a wolf among the sheep," Gabe replied archly.

Lavery was intent on calling the convoy a herd of cows. Several anxious minutes passed then. "She's firing, sir," the lookout bellowed down, "She's firing."

Gabe winced as balls moaned through the air.

"He fired too high," Dagan commented, used to taking prizes not fighting ship to ship.

"Well, his next one won't be too high, I bet," Gabe replied. "Mr Hazard, prepare to fire, sir." Gabe stood up on the small poop deck. The corvette was now not two hundred yards away. "Fire! Give him what for, lads, fire."

SeaWolf's six-pounders spoke as one. Hours of gun drill had paid off.

"She's hit," Dagan replied.

"Down, down everyone," Hazard called and as he did the corvette fired again. Raising himself from the deck, Gabe was stupefied. Twelve guns had fired from the corvette, an entire broadside but with little damage.

"Grape," the master replied, "She's fired with grape."

BOOM!...

SeaWolf gave a shudder; Druett had her guns in action again.

"We're hitting her, Cap'n," Hazard was saying, "She got gaps in her bulwark, spars and rigging are dangling from aloft, and at least two guns are out of order."

Before Hazard had finished his comments the corvette fired again. This time the blast was thunderous. Some of the balls hit the sea and caused fountains of water to gush up on *SeaWolf's* deck. However, some were more effective. Pieces of bulwark were gone, the corner of the small poop deck over Gabe's cabin was blasted away and the gaff boom was shot into. Surveying the damage, Gabe saw Hazard trying to raise himself. Several large splinters had penetrated his coat and were sticking out of his arm. His blue coat was turning dark, then red from the shoulder down his sleeve.

BOOM!...

Druett's gunners were still at work. "We've opened up her gallery, sir."

"Dagan, see to Everette. Mr Lavery, take over for the first lieutenant and prepare to come about."

"Aye, sir."

"Mr Graf, how are things going with the *Lancaster* and *Wild Goose?*"

"*Lancaster's* holding her own, sir, but the corvette seems to be on a course to give *Wild Goose* what for. They beat off the other schooner."

"Well, we'll be there to help directly. Signal the *Lancaster* to maintain her station."

"Mr Dover!"

"Here, Cap'n."

"What's the damage?

"Nothing below decks, sir, me mate's double checking. Most appears to be about the poop and gaff and that don't hinder our sailing. A few shot holes in the sails."

"Deck there, *Wild Goose* just took a broadside from the corvette but then cut across her stern and give her a load up the arse."

"Hell's fire, damned if Estes don't know his business. How are we, Mr Blake?"

"We're over-hauling fast, Cap'n."

"Mr Druett, soon as you think reasonable see if you can get one of the forward guns in action."

"Aye, sir."

"How's the *Lancaster?*"

"She don't look as bad as the schooner, sir. She looks like she's lost her bowsprit and foretopsail.

BOOM!…

"Druett's got a gun in action, sir."

"Deck there, the corvette's hauling her wind, sir. So has the schooner."

"Wear ship, Mr Lavery, let's see about that other schooner."

"Aye, sir, bosun hands to braces."

"Dagan, how is Mr Hazard?"

"Caleb's taking care of him. Mr Davy helped me get him below deck and he said to the first lieutenant, "don't worry, Mr Hazard, the surgeons got plenty of experience with splinters, see here", then the bugger pulled up his shirt and showed Lieutenant Hazard his scar. When he did, Mr Hazard fainted. I wondered if it was from his wound or the scare Davy gave him."

"Cap'n," Lavery was calling, "We're almost on the schooner. She's trying to change tack, but her rigging is in disarray and she's having a hard time of it."

"Where's *Lancaster*?"

"She's on station with the convoy but has requested to give chase."

"Signal stay on station, then signal convoy to heave to. Signal *Wild Goose* to take station to leeward."

"Aye, Cap'n."

"Mr Lavery, put up a flag of truce but have the larboard guns manned and ready. Dagan, get my gig ready. Mr Graf, prepare a boarding party, please."

"Aye, Cap'n."

"Mr Lavery, I intend to board the schooner alone under a flag of truce but if you smell a rat, let loose with a broadside. I'll not endanger any more of our people."

***

The schooner struck her colours without another shot being fired, which was the sensible thing to do. After a thorough search of the prize, Graf said, "Cap'n, she ain't got enough powder to blow fleas offen a cat's arse and very few balls left."

"That's the answer," Gabe replied. "That's why we didn't take much of a beating from the corvette. She didn't have enough powder and ball to take the convoy."

"Then why attack it," Lavery asked.

"A ruse, sir, something to keep us occupied while that damn Patrick got away with the thing they needed most, powder and shot. I'm sure it was only by accident the schooner was disabled. However, she's a small price to pay if we don't get the *Turtle* back with all she carries."

Gabe then called Captain Bruce and being prudent, had the master come along as well as Estes and his first lieutenant for a conference on board *SeaWolf*. He had set Dover to work repairing the schooner.

"We'll divide the prisoners up between our three ships," Gabe told his audience. "Captain Estes, since your lieutenant is the most experienced we'll put him in temporary command of the *Swan*, as nice a prize as we could hope for. He should make do with thirty men and we'll divide those from among each of us. Once the *Swan* is ready to sail I want you, Captain Estes, to take the convoy into Charlestown and unless otherwise ordered wait on me, and then we'll proceed on as ordered."

"Oh…ah…Captain Estes, unless it's put directly to you, say as little as possible about the *Swan*. Have her anchor as close to seaward as possible. Use her boats to unload prisoners if need be."

"Is there a reason for this?" Estes asked.

"Yes, to be quite frank with you. We need her and I'd rather Lord Anthony have first dibs on her before some other admiral snares her."

"I see," Estes said, "But where are you heading that makes it necessary for me to go on with the convoy?"

"I'm going after the *Turtle,* sir. We need that gunpowder and I aim to see we get it back or destroy it and if possible make her captain pay for his treachery."

After Gabe bid his fellow captains farewell, Dagan asked, "Is the schooner, *Swan,* for His Lordship or Markham?"

"Are they not one and the same," Gabe replied raising his eyebrows and giving a hint of a smile.

"Mr Blake, Mr Lavery."

"Aye, Cap'n."

"Attend me in my cabin if you will."

"Aye, sir."

As they entered the cabin, Dawkins asked, "A glass of wine, sir?"

"Yes, Dawkins, I believe we owe ourselves a bit of refreshment."

"Would you like the wine before or after your tea, sir?"

"Damn you, Dawkins, don't you forget anything? I should have left you ashore. Why don't you take that damnable stuff?"

"Cause, sir, the doctor said it was for you and who am I, poor sailor that I be, to argue with the good doctor?"

"You're a damned old rich skinflint, that's what you are. You got more prize money than you know what to do with. Poor—huh."

"Before or after, sir?"

"After, after, damn your eyes, after. Maybe the wine will help wash away the bitterness."

"That's possible, sir, aye, that's possible."

After Gabe took his tea and chased it with half a glass of wine he said, "Not a word from either of you or you'll have it daily instead of your rum ration, now let's get to business. I want to catch the *Turtle* and she's already got a good hour on us. Now, we last saw her heading in a southerly direction. What are your recommendations, Mr Blake?"

Chapter Seven

By two bells in the first dogwatch, repairs had been made to the prize, and the convoy was away on a northerly heading for Charlestown. *SeaWolf* had sailed west-sou-west. The light was going fast and visibility was low when Dagan came down from the masthead lookout. He'd been perched there for an hour now scanning the horizon, occasionally putting the glass to his eye for a clearer picture. The regular lookout had tried to engage Dagan in conversation for the first several minutes they shared the platform. These attempts stopped suddenly when Dagan gave the man a stern look and said, "I'm looking for a ship, not conversation, now put your glass to work."

Gabe had just about given up on sighting his quarry when Dagan approached him. "I found her." Gabe had the master, Blake, and Lieutenant Hazard meet with him in his cabin to go over Dagan's finding on the chart.

"There're some small islands here with a small inlet between them. The *Turtle* is about here."

"That's Hunting Islands," the master offered. "There're about five little islands that make up the Huntings. The *Turtle*, if it's between this northernmost small island and larger one, the main Hunting Island, then she's in the Warsaw Sound."

"The Hunting Islands down to Jenkins Island," Blake pointed to a small island just off the entrance to

Port Royal Harbour, "along with the sound are greatly affected by the tide. When the tide is out there's mud flats and saw grass all the way to Port Royal. There're a few channels that can be made with a shallow draft barge or ship's boat and I expect that's how they unload such vessels."

"Just how far could a body make it overland?" Hazard asked the master as he peered at the charts.

"At low tide?"

"Aye," Hazard replied, "At low tide."

"If you didn't stick up to arse-hole and elbows in the mud you could walk from the beach at Hunting all the way to Port Royal. Course there are gators and moccasins and varmints that if they don't eat ya or pison ya they'll sting you to death. No, don't be thinking of no land action. It's a boat action or naught," the master stated definitely.

""What do we know about location and depths of the channels?" Gabe asked the master.

"Next to nothing, sir. I know they exist and that's about it."

"Well," Gabe responded, "We don't want to go to Port Royal, just to the inlet here."

"My recommendation," Blake said, "is to wait till it's dark and send a couple boats and cut her out if need be, but I'd rather just go within cannon ball range and blast her."

"The master's got a point," Dagan volunteered.

"But we need that powder, don't we, sir," Hazard interjected.

This brought looks from both Dagan and the master. Seeing the looks, Gabe came to the young lieutenant's aid, "We do need the powder, so here's what we'll do."

***

The boats were put over the side. Mr Davy with the marine sergeant and a squad of his marines, Lieutenant Lavery with his party; then Gabe and Dagan with a group in his gig. Before leaving, Gabe talked with his first lieutenant.

"I know you feel it's your place to go, Everette, but with your arm the way it is that's an impossibility. Besides I need someone here who can handle *SeaWolf* if something goes amiss. I'm not going to sacrifice all those men for one renegade. If I can cut *Turtle* out, I will. If not, I'll make an attempt to blow her up. If that's not feasible, I'll send up a flare. That's your cue to come in and pick us up. Then we'll let Mr Druett and his bunch have some target practice."

"Aye, sir. I'll be ready with *SeaWolf* regardless which plans unfolds."

Then Gabe was quite serious. "There's a letter in my desk drawer for my brother and my mother should I fail to return. Give them both to my brother."

"Aye, sir, but I'm sure that won't be necessary."

Pausing before he climbed down to his gig, Gabe looked over *SeaWolf*. He could never ask for a better ship. She was more than he ever dreamed, a dream that came true in part due to his brother. Yes, his brother, not his half-brother, just his brother. Then as he turned, he felt dizziness overtake him and he had to grasp the bulwark to steady himself. Dagan reached out and touched him.

"Let's just stand off and blast the bugger, Gabe. You're in no shape for what we're about."

Looking at the man who'd been his constant companion for as long as he could remember, Gabe felt a lump in his throat. "I have to Dagan. It's what's expected…it's my duty. Besides I have you with me."

Then as Gabe made his way down the ladder to his gig, Dagan muttered, "Duty be damned, it's you I care about."

Just being in the open water seemed to clear Gabe's dizziness. The air had a slight chill and that seemed to help as well. Tiny wavelets lapped at the sides of the boat as the men put their backs to the oars. It was a hard enough pull just from the distance, but with the ebb tide the pull was even harder.

After thirty minutes of rowing Gabe called a halt and let the men rest. "Everything well, Mr Davy, Lieutenant Lavery."

"Aye," they both responded from their respective boats.

"We'll let the men rest for five minutes, and then we'll start again."

"Aye sir."

The rowing had resumed and after ten minutes a seaman made his way back to where Gabe was sitting next to Dagan at the tiller. Men groaned and cursed as a few toes were bruised at the man's awkward movements.

"Sorry, sir, but I didn't want to speak too loud but they's a light just off the starboard bow, looks like someone's got aholt o' a lanthorn and is walking down the side of a ship."

Dagan put the tiller over and the light was visible and appeared to be moving along the deck of a ship. Davy and Lavery's boats had eased up along side of Gabe's.

"Unless I'm mistaken, gentlemen, yonder lays our missing cow."

This brought a smile from Lavery.

"Let's muffle our oars, then Dagan and I will come up on her starboard quarter astern. Mr Davy, put your boat under her stern but where you'll see my signal. Mr Lavery, I want you to swing wide and, if there's no guard boat or sentry, come up along her bow. Make sure nobody has a loaded musket or pistol. Remember this ship is loaded to the gills with powder and munitions. Any questions? Now let's take our stations and pay attention to my signals."

As the crews put their backs into it, the distant ship became more visible. It was undoubtedly the *Turtle*, her sails were furled and a glow seemed to move about on the weather deck, the lookout with the lanthorn. The larboard side was not visible from this position but Gabe could make out a list to the larboard.

"She's aground…stuck in the bloody mud by damn," he whispered to Dagan.

"Aye, probably beached her on the low tide to unload her," Dagan answered. "I'll bet they got boats in the water working back and forth from the shore now."

"I agree," Gabe turned to the boat crew, "Let's be about it men."

The boats eased their way up to the unsuspecting ship. Voices could be heard on deck. Once, one of the men on board the *Turtle* spit over the side just missing the gig. Gabe was now able to pick out individual faces in the lanthorn light. The same light that helped the men see on the deck also took away their night vision and made it easier for the men in the boats to go unseen. A seaman reached up and grasped hold to *Turtle*.

"Boats as secure as I can make it, sir, without tying off to sumthin'."

The hull was moist and smelled of salt and tar mixed with the distinct odour of mud. As Gabe climbed silently up the side of the ship more men were in evidence on *Turtle's* deck. Barrels of gunpowder filled the deck where they'd been brought up from the hole.

A voice with a distinct Irish brogue said, "Keep that lanthorn away from the barrels you fool. That's gunpowder."

Patrick, the bastard, is on board, Gabe thought, recognizing the voice.

"When's the boats coming back?" one of the men asked.

"We're never gonna get this stuff unloaded by daybreak."

Dagan was standing in the boat as Gabe eased his way back down into the gig.

"Patrick is there and his bosun is by the larboard rail. Two other men are on deck sitting by several barrels of gunpowder, and from the sounds one or two more men are down in the hold."

"Mr Lavery is latched onto the anchor cable sir, and Davy's waiting on your signal." Dagan informed Gabe.

"Very well, let's be about it."

As Gabe climbed back up *Turtle's* hull he was suddenly met face to face with the man who'd spit over the side just minutes before. Then everything happened at once. Seeing a British officer rise up startled the man as he spat. He instinctively grabbed Gabe and bellowed, "What the hell?"

Gabe was bodily swung over the bulwark and thrown across the deck landing with a thud, almost at Patrick's feet. Quick to recover himself, Gabe rose up and grabbed Patrick with one hand as he tried to get the handle of his sword in his other hand. It was dangling from his wrist by its lanyard. Hearing the shout and commotion on deck behind him, the man who was holding the lanthorn and peering down to where the boats were being loaded was startled. As he swung around he banged the lanthorn on a stanchion, shattering it and sending the flaming candle across the deck and into the barrels of gunpowder. The clumsy sailor was wild-eyed with fright. In moving the barrels of gunpowder in such haste a stave had separated and grains of powder had leaked out of a barrel and lay upon the deck.

The rolling candle sparked a few grains that then caused a larger flash.

Seeing this, the doomed man said, "Oh hell!" They were the last words he uttered.

Captain Patrick's back was to the flash, but he saw the reflection in Gabe's eyes. "My God!" he screamed. The explosion was tremendous. The ship, the inlet, and the sky all seemed to burst apart and a great flame shot up in the air twenty feet or more lighting up the night sky. Then everything came raining down; bodies, water, and fiery debris.

Men were dead and floating in the water. Others were temporarily blinded and deaf from the explosion, blood draining from their ears and nose. Some suffered burns while others were thankful they were unharmed.

Surprisingly, *SeaWolf's* boats would all float even though they'd overturned with the explosion. The boats were righted, water was bailed out and sailors helped their wounded mates into the boats. Those who could swam the short distance to the muddy shore. Lieutenant Lavery and Mr Davy were each in a boat.

"Where's the Cap'n?" Lavery asked.

"He was on deck," Davy replied.

"Then he's gone," Lavery responded.

"No…he's alive," Dagan almost shouted. "Let's search for him."

"He's gone, Dagan," Lavery said putting his hand on Dagan's shoulder.

"He's alive."

"No one could live through that, Dagan."

"He's alive."

Lavery looked to Davy for support but got none.

"Maybe he is alive," Davy said, remembering events involving Lieutenant Witzenfeld and the pirate captain when they'd been on *Drakkar*. "Dagan's usually right," he added, "And it can't hurt to look."

"All right," Lavery knew it was futile to argue and truthfully he didn't want to argue with Dagan. The piercing look he'd gotten from Dagan when he said the captain was gone sent a shiver clean through his body. His eyes seemed to penetrate clear to his soul and made him feel weak. No, it wouldn't hurt to look but he'd send up a flare for *SeaWolf*, not that one was needed. If they didn't see the explosion there wasn't much need sending up a flare.

"Mr Lavery," one of the bosun's mates was calling. "We got visitors from both directions."

SeaWolf was just off shore and a group of colonials were on the beach.

"Put a white flag on an oar and let's see if they know anything about the captain," Lavery told the bosun mate.

With a piece of torn white shirt tied to an oar, Lavery was rowed over to the beach where a crowd of colonials and slaves were gathered. As the boat ground into the mud one of the slaves pulled it further up onto the beach. Lavery and Dagan got out of the boat. Some of the colonials looked ready to fight.

"Why'd you blow up the ship?" one of the better dressed men asked.

Before Lavery could speak, Dagan replied, "We didn't. It happened just as we arrived." This caused a few hushed whispers.

"What are you looking for?" Again this from the better dressed man. As he spoke, he tapped sand from his boot with a walking stick.

"Our captain," Lavery said not wanting it to appear that Dagan was in charge. "He'd just gone on board the ship when it exploded."

"Then he's dead!" one of the men said toward the back of the crowd.

"We've found no body," Lavery said.

"Ain't likely to either," again the man in back spoke.

Dagan, however, was paying no attention to the man. He was looking at one of the slaves. He looked familiar, he knew him, but from where? The man had looked him in the eye but only for a moment. Dagan couldn't make eye contact with him again. To do so deliberately in front of the colonials would probably cost the slave his life.

As more of *SeaWolf's* boats approached, the colonials turned to walk away. The neatly dressed man paused. "I'm sorry for your captain. I hope you find him." Then like the others he walked over the dune into the brush and out of sight.

Back on board *SeaWolf*, Dagan, Dawkins, and Caleb sat with Lieutenant Hazard in Gabe's cabin. "The captain left instructions and letters before he left for the cutting out. I'm sure you know about them Dagan. Anyway, I'm to pick up the convoy in Charlestown, and then go on to New York and Philadelphia. Then find Lord Anthony's squadron. That's what I intend to do unless otherwise instructed."

"You won't be," Dagan responded, then added, "I'll give Lord Anthony the letters. He has to know Gabe's alive."

Hazard wanted to say something but couldn't find the words. Maybe it was better to let Dagan go on hoping. Maybe that was his way to deal with his loss.

"I have to go on deck. You gentlemen finish your wine."

No mention had been made of changing his things into the captain's cabin. It wasn't the right time. It would only be temporary Hazard knew. His Lordship certainly had someone more qualified than him for *SeaWolf*, but he'd enjoy the chance to command while it lasted. On his way on deck Hazard thought of his last meeting with Gabe. He called me Everette, he thought. Not Lieutenant Hazard but Everette.

PART TWO

Sailor's Farewell

The day is dark and dreary
I can smell the rain
I'm sailing with the tide
Will I stand the pain
Teary-eyed she waves goodbye
Watching as I go
It's a conflict of emotion
Waging war in my soul

…Michael Aye

Chapter One

It's a fine Navy day is it not, Mr Oxford?" Lord Anthony greeted *Warrior's* master.

"Aye, My Lord, it promises to be just that, long as we keep our distance from yonder island."

The winds had been perverse and after two days of a northern gale Anthony could understand the master's apprehensions.

Patrolling the frigid water from Nantucket to Halifax and back was bad enough, but to be pushed onto the rocks in a heavy gale would likely mean certain death.

Sable Island lay off the larboard beam. In the years since 1750, both the French and British navy had lost all manner of ships, from third rates to brigs, off Sable's treacherous waters.

"Morning, My Lord!"

Turning, Anthony greeted his flag captain, "'Morning, Dutch."

Captain Moffett had strolled up to the windward side of the quarterdeck to greet his admiral. Rightfully this space belonged to Moffett by tradition but old habits died hard. How many times had Lord Anthony paced this area on his own ship? Moffett couldn't recall ever hearing of a captain confronting an admiral over where he could or couldn't pace on his flagship.

"Has our flock returned to the mother hen, Dutch?"

"Aye, My Lord, *Pigeon* and *Audacity* have returned on station. *Merlin* and *Drakkar* were able to keep station during the gale."

Merlin...Buck, steady Mr Buck, now a captain in command of his own ship. Anthony had never known a more reliable man. And Pope, who was now captain on *Drakkar,* had proven himself time and time again fighting pirates in the West Indies.

Lieutenant Harold Kerry in command of *Pigeon* and Lieutenant George Bush in command of *Audacity* were unknowns. They both seemed capable seaman but neither had the experience of Steve Earl, Gabe, or even Markham.

Realizing Moffett had spoken Anthony replied, "I'm sorry, Dutch, my mind is adrift today."

Moffett had sensed Lord Anthony was worried. Lieutenant Anthony and *SeaWolf* should have been back weeks ago. That combined with running before the gale for two days had increased Lord Anthony's anxiety.

"I was saying sir, I wouldn't be surprised if 'young Gabe'—as Bart was so apt to call Lieutenant Anthony—didn't get sent on some errand by Lord Howe."

"That's possible," Anthony replied without conviction.

Changing tack Moffett continued, "With your permission, My Lord, I'd thought I'd have the bosun pipe 'make and mend.' After the wetting we took from the gale the crew could use the time to patch things up and dry out some clothes."

"I agree, Dutch, but it's your ship. You don't need my permission for your daily routine."

"Thank you, My Lord, here comes your cox'n."

Anthony watched as his cox'n approached. Another reliable man. "Damme, Bart, but you appear more like a senior officer than I do dressed in your cox'n coat."

"It's the one yews picked out, sir, and glad I am of it. It be much colder here than at 'ome."

"I agree," Anthony replied. "Now tell me, Bart, what's so urgent to have you moving before the forenoon watch?

"Breakfast."

"Breakfast?"

"Aye, sir, Silas done said to hurry on down afore the eggs get cold."

"He does, does he?"

"Aye, sir, iffen yews to be awhile, we uns will dispose of 'em and Silas will set to cooking yews some more."

"Uh huh! And am I to understand that by disposing of the eggs means the two of you will eat them?"

"At's one way of disposing of 'em, I guess, now yews mentioned it. Hit would be sinful to waste 'em."

"Well, go dispose of them as you and Silas see fit, but tell Silas I'll be there directly and if I don't have a hot breakfast he'll taste the cats, a dozen at least"

"Aye, Cap'n, oh aye, sir, taste the cat he will, ha! ha!, and I'll count the lashes for you, I will."

"Count the lashes, you old dog, you couldn't count past ten with your boots off."

"That may be true, sir, but I's bettin old Silas'd never last more'n 'alf a dozen. That's me wager."

As always Bart had spoken the last word, then had gone.

***

Anthony had finished his eggs and was on his second cup of coffee when the marine announced, "Flag lieutenant, zur."

"Gunfire," Markham exclaimed as he burst into the cabin.

"Are you sure?" Anthony questioned.

"Aye, My Lord."

Trying not to appear too excited, Anthony made his way on deck with Markham and Bart in tow.

Captain Moffett had a glass to his eye peering at the group of sails just on the horizon. Sensing someone was near, Moffett acknowledged his admiral. "Sorry, My Lord, my mind was on yonder sail."

"As is mine," Anthony replied, "Have you been able to sort it out?"

"Aye, sir, it appears to be the convoy. We think the rear of the convoy is being harassed by those damn colonial raiders. We patrol for weeks and not a sight, but just as soon as the convoy arrives so do the sharks."

"No point in showing, less there's bounty to be had, is there, Dutch?"

"No, My Lord, but it's vexing all the same."

About that time the lookout hailed down. "*Merlin's* up to the head of the convoy, sir, but I can't make out what's happening further back in the pack."

Anthony looked to Moffett upon hearing the lookout's report.

"I sent *Merlin* and *Audacity* to investigate as they were closest to convoy," Moffett stated. "I'm sure those raiders will be less likely to hang around if there's a show of force."

"Good," Anthony replied.

Half an hour later the first of the convoy were clearly visible and headed to Halifax. Lieutenant Angus approached the first lieutenant, "Have you noticed, sir, how all the ships in the colonies are named. It amazes me. We've seen the *Bonnie Lass*, the *Sarah*, and the *Beloved Brenda*. Do you think she's a wife or mistress?"

"I don't know," Herrod answered Angus, "but keep your eyes peeled for the *Charming Peggy*. She's been turned into a privateer."

Hearing the Lieutenant's talk of wives and mistresses made Anthony think not only of his wife, Lady Deborah, but also of his father's mistress and Gabe's mother, Maria. Deborah and his sister, Becky, had vowed to visit Maria frequently. Anthony could only imagine how alone she must feel living in the house in Portsmouth. Her companion of many years now gone, and her son far away fighting in the war. Anthony prayed all was well. He also prayed Deborah was well. She was his wife, his friend, and his lover. She was all a woman should be. She had been very proud of Anthony's promotion, but on their last night together before the squadron sailed, she had whispered, "Admiral you'll be to the world, but to me you'll always by my dashing captain."

She'd wanted to be left with child. "Your leaving will be almost unbearable," she'd said.

"I'll worry everyday, but if I'm with child, I believe, it would be much easier." Deborah was nearly thirty while Anthony was thirty-eight. Neither were old, but old enough. Waiting would only worsen the risk for Deborah, Caleb had said. Well, if she were not with child it would not be from lack of trying. If she was, Anthony wondered when he would be home to see his child. How old would he or she be? God! So much to ponder.

"Deck there!" the lookout again. "*Merlin* has come about and is headed our way. Looks like she's got a small prize."

Anthony turned to his flag captain, "Signal, have captain repair on board, once the rest of the convoy is up with us, Dutch."

"Aye, My Lord."

"Bart!"

"Here, sir."

"Let's go on down and get out of the captain's way. We're taking up space like gear adrift. It's not quite noon yet, but I think a glass of wine might be refreshing."

Bart muttered a reply, but Anthony didn't hear it due to the bosun yelling at some oaf for banging a bucket of water and spilling it on the deck.

"I'm sorry, Bart, what did you say?"

Looking somewhat sheepish, Bart answered, "Me said, it's bound to be noonish sumwheres."

Chapter Two

Anthony was on *Warrior's* deck when *SeaWolf* took station just to windward of the flagship. Anthony immediately noticed the ship handling was not the smooth crisp seamanship Gabe normally demonstrated. Then, when he saw Lieutenant Hazard and Dagan being rowed over, he knew something terrible was wrong. He felt his chest tighten and he became nauseated. It was hard to catch his breath. Bart also knew something was amiss and his experienced eye picked out the various repairs that had been conducted on *SeaWolf* as a result of battle.

Moving up close, Bart touched Anthony's arm without being conspicuous. "Let's go below, sir, Cap'n Moffett can talk with Mr Hazard. That way Dagan can come on downs to us uns."

Anthony felt half in a trance when he gave Moffett the order to keep Lieutenant Hazard occupied until he sent for him. Then he made his way to his cabin.

***

"He's alive, My Lord. I feel it in my bones...my soul. I don't want you to listen to Hazard, Lavery, or any of them," Dagan said addressing Anthony in his day cabin. "He may be hurt or a captive, but he's alive."

Dagan had told the entire story as Anthony, Markham, Bart, and Silas sat and listened without interruption, drinks untouched in their hands.

"This slave, you say you recognized him?"

"Aye," Dagan replied. "At first, I couldn't place him, but then it come to me. The man who let Commodore Gardner use his house at English Harbour."

"Mr Montique?"

"Adam Montique," Markham added.

"Aye, that's him. It was his slave and I believe he was there on the beach. I didn't get a look at him because he was in the back of the group of men that had gathered, but I'm sure it was him. He kept saying Gabe was a goner, but I felt different. I was torn between leaving the ship there and searching for Gabe or coming here to speak with you, then going back and fetching him home. I didn't want any trouble with Mr Hazard. I knew you'd have enough troubles without me causing more by hurting the young lieutenant's feelings by jumping ship or disobeying his orders."

"So what do you plan?" Anthony asked.

"I'd like to go to Petersburg in Virginia. That's where my uncle is and I believe he can get me back to Port Royal."

"Why not take a ship?" Markham asked, not able to restrain himself.

"Anyone seeing the ship would know who we are and likely know what we were about before we could get close enough to do any good."

"Who do you want to take with you?" Anthony asked.

Dagan could see Bart and Markham were ready to go but said, "Caleb. He talks and sounds like a colonial and he's known to some. If anyone else came it would only slow us down."

Then looking at Markham but addressing Anthony, Dagan said, "The prize we took, the *Swan*, Gabe was hoping you'd take her in and maybe give her to Mr Markham."

"Did he?" Anthony said, unable to hide a smile even with the heaviness he felt over Gabe's disappearance. Then turning to his flag lieutenant he said, "Well, Gabe's right, Francis. It's time you were given a ship. The choice is yours. You can have *Swan* or you can take command of *SeaWolf*. Understanding either is only temporary for now."

"I'll take *Swan*, sir. It was in Gabe's mind when he took her that she'd be mine, so I feel she's the one I ought to have. Besides, sir, I wouldn't want to take away *SeaWolf* from Lieutenant Hazard."

Anthony looked at Markham, "You wouldn't be. He's too junior and inexperienced for command. If you take *Swan*, I'm going to put Steve Earl in temporary command of *SeaWolf* until we get Gabe back. Hopefully, Earl will have his own command soon, but for now it's *SeaWolf*. Now, go pack your chest and make a list of anyone special you'd like to have. I'm not sure about a lieutenant but a senior midshipman and a good master's mate. Ask Mr Oxford if you don't have anyone in mind."

"Only one, sir."

"Just one?" Anthony queried.

"Aye, My Lord. I'd like Mr Davy if possible but no one else in particular."

"Very well, he's yours. Now on your way up pay my respects to Captain Moffett and have him and Lieutenant Hazard come down as soon as convenient."

"Silas."

"Aye, My Lord."

"Do you think you can round up Vally, Captain Moffett's clerk, and the two of you give us a legible set of orders?"

"Aye, My Lord, we'll see to it, us uns will."

While waiting on the clerks to draw up the orders for Lieutenant Markham and Lieutenant Earl, Anthony listened quietly as Lieutenant Hazard gave his report. After finishing his report of the explosion and Gabe's disappearance, Hazard went on to tell of a chance meeting with the brig of war, *HMS Hatchet*.

"Her captain told me after Admiral Parker had failed to take Sullivan's Island, the fleet hauled their wind."

"What of Lord Clinton?" Captain Moffett interrupted.

"I'm not sure, sir. I caught up with the convoy and sailed on to Norfolk. There's still a large British presence there but there's also open defiance and unrest. I then sailed on to New York after a brief skirmish just off the coast at Philadelphia. I spoke with Admiral Graves at New York, sir, and I have his messages for you. His flag lieutenant told me the admiral is in a state of humours about how things are going in the southern colonies and in Philadelphia as well."

"Did the admiral say anything about the *Swan*?" Lord Anthony asked.

"No sir, but I wrote my report in such haste I may have forgot to mention her, sir."

Hearing this Moffett slapped his knee and crowed, "Well, damme, this boy's got promise, My Lord."

Before dismissing Hazard, Anthony explained why he was putting Lieutenant Earl in temporary command of *SeaWolf*. "Your day will come and when it does I'll not forget your loyalty."

Chapter Three

Along the beach, a young girl and her nanny search for shells.

"Bring that lanthorn closer here, Nanny, how am I to see if you're standing so far up on the beach."

"Huh, child! You don't need to be sashaying down there in dem dark waters. You can't see nothing and one dem whales'll be done come up heah and swollered you."

"Well, I certainly can't see if you keep the lanthorn so far up on the beach. Now Sarah Livingston comes here at night and she's got three big conch shells. I want at least six. She's always so prissy. Did you see how low her dress was in front the other night? Made that Luke Tarlton's eye bulge. If she'd took a deep breath, her ninnies would have popped out for sure."

"Hush, child, how you talk. Yo blessed mother would have me washing yo mouth out with lye soap if she hadn't done gone on to be with da angels. Now get on up here."

"Oh, Nanny, ain't no whale going to come up on this beach and swallar me. Uncle Adam said a whale hasn't got a mouth big enough to swallow a man."

"He don't, do he! Well, you jus tell that to po' old brother Jonah, what be in the Bible. He done got swallowed by de whale. 'Sides, iffen a whale don't getcha wonna dem crocogators what Mr Hindley talks about will. Now come on. You already done got foh o' dem shells. Dat's one moh than dat nasty Sarah done got. You knows I told Lum we wouldn't be long when he fetched us over here in dat boat. You knows dat Mr Hindley will give Lum what foh iffen we's get caught. Lawd, I don't knows how I let myself get talked into yo shenanigans. Huh! Cause I loves ya, I guess and I gave my solemn word to yo blessed momma foh she went onto Jesus."

"Nanny!"

"Yes, child."

"Are you sweet on Uncle Lum?"

"Hush, child, LAWD!! What foolishness. What was that?"

"It was some kind of explosion, Nanny."

"We ain't being attacked by dem Britishers is we girl?"

"No, Nanny, but something blew up. What did Uncle Lum say they was unloading off that ship, Nanny? Was it gunpowder?"

"I don't know child, but we's got to hurry along now. Lum will be worried sho 'nuff."

***

All was still in the predawn hours. The inlet was bathed in moonlight and like giant fireflies pieces of burning debris would flicker on the receding waters then hiss as the tide carried it on. Then the smoke seemed to roll in with a faint offshore breeze. Gabe opened his eyes. It took a moment for them to adjust to the blackness before him. His ears were ringing. He hurt. He was lying flat in a foul smelling mud. He could smell smoke as it came in off the water. The salt from the sea, the mud, and the smoke, all of these odors seemed to fill his nostrils and burn his lungs as he tried to breathe.

His service coat was plastered to him. The sleeves were singed and blackened. He rolled over to his back. God it hurt, but his breathing seem to be easier. It was only when he moved he felt the sharp pains in his ribs, probably broken. He felt the tide as it rushed past his head, some going in his ears and causing him to shake his head to clear them. He had felt numb but now his feelings must be returning. He could feel the cold with the wet and caked mud. Lying there, he went over what happened in his mind.

He was lucky to be alive. Luck. His hand went to the leather pouch tied around his neck. His luck. The ruby was still there in its pouch. He turned back over onto his stomach and even though it hurt he half-crawled, half-slithered through the mud and seaweed up toward the beach. He must have passed out because he suddenly heard voices, female voices and footsteps. Gabe panicked, tried to crawl faster, but now not only did his ribs hurt but so did his leg. Afraid to feel but also afraid not to, Gabe reached down and found a gash in his leg. *Damn*, he thought again, *an open wound and crawling around in this muck. If he didn't get help he'd surely lose his leg if not die.*

Friends? Could they be loyalists? As soon as the idea occurred common sense told him otherwise. The voices and footsteps grew louder. Loyalist or colonial, he needed help.

"Help!" It was hardly more than a whisper. Gabe clinched his teeth against the pain as he tried to raise himself. Impatience gripped him and with all his strength he shoved his body forward and gasped, "Help!"

"What's that?"

"What's what?"

"Over there, Nanny, look."

"Come back heah child. I don't want you et up by no crocogator."

"Oh!" Gabe let out a groan.

"It's a man, Nanny. Now get over here with that lanthorn." Faith had never spoken with such firmness before, so Nanny hurried over. Gabe lay there, the pain had once more taken his consciousness.

"Help me, Nanny, let's get him up on the sand outta that mud." As Gabe was pulled up on the sand Faith turned to Nanny, "Go get Uncle Lum and tell him we got a hurt man. Get back here quickly now. I'll stay with him till you get back."

Realizing that there was no point in arguing, Nanny did as she was told but muttered as she went back. "Jus like her mama, always coming up with a stray."

"Oh…Oh!" Gabe groaned twice as he tried to sit up. Without a lanthorn to see the man's wounds, Faith did as much as she could to comfort him by tearing off a lower portion of her dress and wiping the mud and debris from his face. She then sat down on the sand and helped the man sit up by holding him. This also would help warm him. His body seemed chilled and he was shaking.

"Who are you?" the man asked in a barely audible whisper.

"Faith, Faith Montique. Who are you?"

"Lieutenant Gabe Anthony."

"What are you doing here?" Faith asked.

"Explosion, ship exploded," Gabe uttered.

"What happened, what happened," Faith asked again, but Gabe had become unconscious once more. Faith could see the lanthorn coming down the beach toward her before she could actually see Uncle Lum and Nanny. They had been the only two slaves her mama had kept when her daddy had died. Mother had turned everything over to Uncle Adam, who was her father's brother. Now her mother was gone having succumbed to pneumonia. Uncle Adam was kind but distant and Faith always felt he stared at her like he was undressing her with his eyes. He'd never said anything or touched her, but nevertheless Faith had seen him with the town's women. Also, a few times, Mr Hindley had brought him women off one of the ships. Then after a few days they'd disappeared.

This didn't count all the times Faith had seen young slave girls being taken to his room at night. Sarah Livingston had said she had caught Uncle Adam looking down her bosom, then letting his elbow touch her breast like it was an accident. So far, she hadn't been touched, but she knew it was only time until something happened. She was eighteen and had filled out over the past two years. Nanny would say "you's a child in a woman's body."

***

Getting Gabe back to the boat and loaded on board had been a chore. Uncle Lum followed the channels back going past Lady's Island into the Broad River, then on into Beaufort. Once they landed, Uncle Lum rounded up the mule he'd left hobbled and grazing. Then he hitched up the wagon and with some difficulty got Gabe into the wagon.

"Is he heavy, Uncle Lum?" Faith asked.

Lum was huffing and puffing from the exertion caused by trying to load the unconscious man. "He be heavy, missy, but he's got soggy clothes and boots. Dat don't hep none plus I'm a bit tired rowing dat boat on a tide what be going out. Come on tho, we's got to git foh Mastuh Adam starts asking questions."

Looking up, Faith could see the sun as the fog was breaking. "We should have done been back."

"Yesum, we shoulda, it's gotta be nine o'clock or atter."

By the time they'd made it to the plantation the fog was nearly gone. A little was left swirling about the low lying areas that were so much a part of the area around Beaufort. Spanish moss hung low from the trees on both sides of the road creating a natural canopy. At intervals rays of light would shine through a gap causing the dew on the moss to sparkle. Gabe opened his eyes and caught the view. Looking up at the girl who brushed his face with hands as soft as velvet, he was sure he'd gone to heaven and had an angel before him.

The girl was small and dainty but almost voluptuous. She was tanned yet seemed radiant. A small nose covered with a few freckles that made her look bright and innocent. She had a small provocative mouth but a large, pretty smile showing perfect teeth. Blonde, lustrous hair showed beneath her bonnet. Surely, she was an angel. Had he gone to heaven?

The stiff mule-drawn wagon hit a pothole that caused pain to shoot through Gabe making him cough. No, he hadn't made it to heaven yet.

"Damn, Uncle Lum, must you hit every hole? You killing this poor man." *Well, maybe she wasn't an angel after all*, Gabe thought.

"Hush yo mouth, chile, ain't no use you takin on like Mister Hindley," Nanny fussed. "I hope yo momma wasn't lookin' down at you jus now."

Chapter Four

It had been a quick trip for the *Swan* travelling south from Nova Scotia to Norfolk. Markham was a new man.

"She's a fine ship, Cap'n," a smiling Mr Davy had said when he'd first boarded *Swan*. It was hard for Markham to recall the shy, angry little boy who'd been a fellow midshipman on *Drakkar*. They had both grown and matured under then Captain and now Admiral Anthony.

Markham was happy with all about but still anxious about Gabe. Getting Gabe back would make Markham's world complete again. Dagan had said Gabe was alive. Markham would never question Dagan. He'd seen too much happen in the past to ever doubt Dagan, but still he worried. Markham was sure no one would ever know, but he'd went to Dagan with the idea of "creating an accident" for Lieutenant Witzenfeld when he had been tormenting Mr Davy and Gabe back in the early days on *Drakkar*.

Dagan had put his hand on then midshipman Markham's shoulder that day and quietly but firmly stated, "Mr Witz's time on this earth is nigh, young sir. I thank you for your concern, but it's time the lieutenant gets a taste of his own medicine. Mind you now this is between us. I tell you so you and young Davy don't go getting yourself in trouble." The next day, Witz went mad and jumped overboard.

"Commodore's signal, sir, repair on board."

This broke Markham's thought. "Very well, Mr Harrell. Prepare my gig while Mr Davy gets the dispatch bag. Dagan?"

"Aye, sir."

"Whenever you and Caleb are ready let the bosun know. He has the jolly boat ready with a crew to put you ashore." Dagan could see Markham wanted to say more but the emotion seemed to be building and he was in danger of being overwhelmed by it.

"We'll bring Gabe back, sir," Dagan said to help alleviate the tension.

"You do that, Dagan. Keep Caleb in line and away from the women and wine."

"Aye, sir."

"Dagan?"

"Yes sir?"

"How'd you talk Lord Anthony into keeping the damned ape?"

"It took all I could muster," Dagan replied with a grin on his face, "But in truth Silas and the ape has taken to one another, so maybe everything will be fine till we return."

"Have a safe trip, Dagan, and remind Gabe it's his time to stand a round when he gets back. Now let me be off, Mr Davy, commodores don't like lieutenants keeping them waiting."

***

The decision to allow Caleb along proved fruitful immediately. After supping at a tavern Caleb knew to be frequented by colonials, it was made known Dagan needed to go to Petersburg to visit his uncle and let the uncle know about grave family matters.

"Who be this man in Petersburg you want to see?"

This question was from a man with long hair and a drooping moustache that seem full of food crumbs and grease. He wore a shapeless hat, a worn tattered coat, and a buckskin hunting shirt that was glazed in grease, buckskin leggings and moccasins. He spoke with a twang in his voice.

"His name is Andre," Caleb replied. "Andre Dupree, he raises thoroughbreds outside Petersburg." It had been decided to let Caleb do most of the talking with Dagan speaking only when needed.

At the mention of the name the wiry little man seem to relax. "Name's Frost. Most folks call me Frosty," he said pointing to his hair. "I been gray since I was just a young he coon. Kinda like nature's way of a joke, I guess. Last name be Frost and an early frost on top o' the mountain."

"Are you headed to Petersburg?" Caleb asked.

"Well, I got a might o' freight that needs to go that way soon, I reckon. You ain't no redcoat loyalist, is you?"

"Our loyalty is to our family," Dagan replied, speaking for the first time.

"Well, I guess you'll do," Frosty said, "But I'm warning you, it's not an easy trip. There's bound to be British patrols and them fusiliers shoot furst and ask questions later. Oncet we inland a bit it gets a tad easier."

"How do you get past the guards with freight," Caleb asked. "I'm sure they search every wagon."

"They's do, but who said we's gonna be in a wagon? No, we'd be caught for sure. I got myself a string of mules and packs."

"When do we leave?" Caleb asked.

Frosty eyed the two suspiciously, "Well fer now that's fer me to know and yer to be ready when I calls you. Then you'll know. What I'd recommend is when yer lays yer head down to sleep, has yer things packed case I calls."

***

It was just before dawn when Frosty came for Caleb and Dagan. "Stir yerselves if you wanna go. Better grab yer coats cause it's a might frosty…he! he! he!" The old man chuckled at his own joke. The three made a quiet departure from the inn.

"It's dark," Caleb commented as the frost crunched beneath his feet. "What time do you think it is?"

"I reckon it's about four," Frosty replied, "But let the clock worry about itself and keep quiet." Frosty led them down a slippery path between several buildings and seemingly led them in circles. Finally they found themselves at a tobacco warehouse on the edge of town. Here four mules were tied up with packs already loaded on their backs.

"I wonder what's in those packs," Caleb thought to himself, but knew better than to ask. Then out of nowhere, a cautious voice, "Yer late."

Caleb and Dagan could see the gun in the man's hand. Its barrel positioned just so it covered them.

"Well, we's here and we's ready," Frosty replied. "Them redcoats got patrols everywhere and I had ta take an extra turn or two."

"Well be on your way," the man said handing the lead rope to Frosty. A quick handshake and he vanished into the dawn.

***

The three had travelled about an hour when Dagan could see they were walking along a muddy path just above a river. The animals moved as though they were used to the trail. Frosty had hold of the lead mule's halter rope with his hand patting its nose.

"All right, boys, lets get under cover for a spell," he said as he led the way to a small shed a few yards inland from the river. As the dawn faded, the sky was cloudy and a light sprinkle had started. "Knew it was gonna rain," Frosty commented. "My rheumatism is acting up a might."

"Have you tried a willow bark tea?" Caleb asked. "It's supposed to be good for such agues."

"That a fact," the old man said. "I been nursing my sour mash along and it's done a fair job keeping my aches down."

"Yes, but the willow bark does more than calm the malady. It will quench the humour that inflames the joint."

"How's come you know so much about rheumatism?" Frosty ask.

"I'm a physician, of course," Caleb responded as full of dignity as he could muster.

"Huh!" Frosty snorted. "I done saddled meself with one man who's edumecated and tother that can't rightly speak." Then the old man grinned as a thought entered his head. "What kinda cure ya got fer byils?"

"Byils? What's a byil?" Caleb asked.

"I thought you was a doctor. A byil is a sore. A big sore. I gets 'em on my seat."

"Huh!" Caleb replied, "You mean you get boils, likely from setting on your arse to much. However, the cure is to lance the lesion and drain out the putrefaction. I will sometimes apply a poultice and a wick."

"Well, I ain't got nairn now," Frosty replied, "But next time I do I'll look you up if you's about."

***

The rain got harder as the sky darkened and the wind grew. "It's sure to be a gully washer," Frosty volunteered as he went about taking the packs off the mules. The smell of the wet animals filled the small shed.

As the rain picked up, water began to drip through the roof in places, some dripping down the flank of one of the mules, causing it to stamp its foot and swish its tail. The earthen floor soon started to dampen as well but overall the men were comfortable in the temporary shelter.

After an hour or so the rain dwindled to a mist. Rising from his spot in the corner, Frosty groaned and stretched. "I better go scout out the ferry. If you will, load the mules so we can leave quick as I'm back. That rain has most likely played havoc with the crossing, so we need to be quick about it afore the blame river swells ta where we can't cross."

As Frosty ducked out the door, Dagan started rubbing the dampness from the mules back in preparation for loading the packs.

"What do you suppose are in those packs?" Caleb asked Dagan.

"I don't know and don't want to know."

"You don't want to know?"

"No."

"Why?"

"Because if we're ever asked I can truthfully say I've never knowingly aided the enemy."

"I'll be damned," Caleb thought seeing Dagan's wisdom.

By the time the mules had been rubbed down good and the packs loaded Frosty was back. He paused just inside the doorway to catch his breath, "They's a British patrol down by the ferry. Whole passel of Hessian by gawd, and they's headed this way so let's skedaddle. We'll circle round and come in from the south. Give 'em Hessians time to clear on out. I just hope the river ain't to swelled to cross by then."

***

For two days after a harrowing raft trip across a flooded river, the trio with their mules wound themselves deeper and deeper into the wilderness. Caleb commented to Dagan at one point when they had stopped to rest, "I'm damn glad he knows where he's going cause I don't."

Overhearing the comment, Frosty replied, "We's on a game trail."

"With these supplies," he said nodding his head toward the mules and packs, "We have to stay off the main trails."

Wild game was abundant. Fish filled the creeks and streams, but Frosty didn't want to waste time fishing. "Take too long," he swore when Caleb brought it up. Once when crossing a small stream, they came across a black bear with yearling cubs. Frosty gave them a wide berth.

"Don't want to lose one of the mules or one of the ewes either," Frosty said off-handedly. On the third day he shot a deer. "Nice fat doe," he said cheerfully, "Bout time we had us some fresh meat."

"You boys ever ate venison?" he asked, as he cut out the back strap and tenderloins. Holding the pieces of meat, Frosty had a gleam in his eye. "This is foh tonight. We'll take the hind quarters for later."

Laying the fresh cut meat on a rock, Frosty then wiped his bloody knife and hands on the legs of his buckskins. Seeing this Caleb couldn't help but shake his head. It wasn't over ten to fifteen feet to the stream where the man could have washed his hands. Oh well, Caleb thought, eyeing the soiled buckskins. What's a little blood compared to what was already on the man's garb. Some of it even seemed to be alive, and since the rain all of it smelled. If Frosty could live with it so could he.

Later, after they had camped and Dagan had filled his belly with roasted venison he lit his pipe and lay down to rest. The camp fire would crackle and small embers would pop into the air only to fall back into the bed of hot coals. An owl hooted in a near by tree and something splashed in the creek not far off. Frosty had let his pipe go out and was relighting it from a burning stick from the fire. Caleb had already lain down. Asleep?

Dagan didn't think so, not by the uneven breaths. Caleb had long, even breaths when he slept. Frosty snored.

Settling on down, Dagan gazed at the stars. Everything seemed too peaceful, so tranquil. It was hard to imagine a war was going on. How was Gabe? Dagan felt tormented not knowing. He knew Gabe was alive, but he couldn't get a better feel for what was going on.

It was impossible to rush Frosty who seemed content with the mules' slow pace. Dagan felt an urgency and wanted to be moving but knew it would do no good to push their guide. He would not be rushed.

It was almost noon the next afternoon when the forest seemed to be less dense. Ahead they could hear voices and then they could see a wagon pulled by oxen pass by. They came out of the woods to a well-used road.

"Yonder lies Petersburg," Frosty said pointing with his musket and that a-way be ya uncle's place. It's not more'n two miles." Shifting his musket, Frosty held out his hands. "I don't usually take ta strangers, 'specially British, but you boys be true gen'men. I hope you find ya kin in good health. You boys been good help and good company and iffen I gets me another byil I'm gonna look ya up, Caleb."

Dagan and Caleb shook the offered hand and thanked Frosty for all his help and generosity.

Watching the old man lead his mules on toward Petersburg, Caleb said to Dagan, "I'll miss the ornery old coot, but not his smell."

"No, I'll not miss his smell either," Dagan said, "But if I was ever in battle I'd like a bunch of his kind on my side. I'd put up with the smell to have such a marksman."

"Aye," Caleb agreed, "Especially if he can cook venison."

Chapter Five

The road soon became less travelled and then turned into a well-used wagon path. After a short while they came upon a fence of stone with woods on the right side of the road and fields to the left.

"We're close," Dagan told Caleb. "This is the same kind of fence we had at home." As they walked up to the yard a hound started barking and running toward the two men, scattering a group of chickens. As the dog approached, Dagan held out the back of his hand and after a few soothing whispers, the dog went back and lay under a huge oak tree.

Uncle Andre had a nice home and the kitchen seemed to be separated from the main house by a breezeway. As nice as the house was it was the barn that caught the visitors' eye. It was a huge two-story building that had been built in the Dutch fashion with open doors at both ends. The rear doors opening into a corral. A lean-to had been built off one side and under it a blacksmith's shop set-up.

Uncle Andre was standing in the barn door with a harness over his shoulder. He wore a battered hat and held a long stemmed white clay pipe. Seeing Dagan, he rushed up to him and gave a great hug.

"My boy, my boy," he kept saying. "You've grown into a man." After the greeting Dagan introduced his uncle to Caleb. After the introductions Andre looked at his nephew.

"I knew you were coming. There's been a raven in the oak there for three days now." Then with a sombre look he asked, "Is there trouble, Dagan?"

"Aye, uncle, there's trouble."

Before the conversation could go any further a young woman called from the house, "Papa! Come quickly, Papa, I can see Kawliga and Jubal coming cross the pasture with a new colt."

Looking at Dagan, Andre said, "We'll talk later but right now we have to attend this colt."

As Andre hurried off, Dagan turned to his friend, "Want to see…" Dagan broke off his question. Caleb was staring at the young lady on the porch. "Caleb, Caleb?"

Finally looking at Dagan, Caleb said, "A goddess. A goddess in the wilderness."

***

After an evening meal of greens, potatoes, roast pork, biscuits, and cherry pie, a sated group sat in the parlour. Dagan had been introduced to his cousins, Jubal and Katheryn. Katheryn, who went by the nickname Kitty, was Caleb's goddess. Small talk filled the room. Finding the new colt had been luck.

"The old mare always wanders off to have her foal," Andre had explained. "Why she can't have them in a clean stall in the barn is besides me."

"Papa," Kitty said, "Queenie had ten puppies this morning. Had them under the back porch steps."

"Puppies," Caleb commented, "I love puppies."

"Do you? Would you like to go see Queenie's puppies?" Kitty asked.

"If you don't mind?" Caleb directed this to Andre.

"No, go ahead," then to Kawliga Andre said, "Get a lanthorn." Andre's way of providing a chaperone, Dagan thought.

As the group left to see the puppies Andre turned to Dagan, "Kitty is starved for companionship since her mother died. We've all been lonely, but it's worse for Kitty. She was only four when the small pox came. Since then her only contact with women folk was when she went to school and now on Sundays at church. I have two squaws to help out but they can't teach her about being a lady."

Getting up from his chair, Andre made his way to the fireplace mantle. He took down two pipes and a canister. "Virginia tobacco," he said as he offered a pipe to Dagan. "Best tobacco in the world." After lighting up, Andre looked solemnly at Dagan, "Jubal's got the gift. He doesn't fully understand it yet. But like with the new colt he knew exactly where to go. Kawliga recognized it first. He calls Jubal little *colonneh*, which in Cherokee means little raven. Say's he'd be a big man in an Indian tribe, a shaman no less."

"How'd Kawliga come about?" Dagan asked.

"We came up on him in the woods one day while hunting. He was sick with fever and about gone. We took care of him and he's been with us since." Then while Kitty was still showing off Queenie's puppies Dagan told his uncle about Gabe. Andre listened without interrupting but nodding at different times. Leaning on the mantle and puffing on their pipes the two men were silent for a few minutes, both in their own thoughts.

Andre broke the silence, "You'll be wanting Jubal and Kawliga to lead you to Port Royal to fetch Gabe, so let's turn in so you can get an early start."

Walking out on the front porch before retiring, Dagan saw Jubal returning from the barn. He'd gone there to check on the colt as soon as the meal had ended, so he'd not heard any of his father and Dagan's conversation.

As he climbed the stone steps to the porch he put out the lanthorn. He then looked at Dagan and said, "I've been yearning for a trip. I reckon you came at the right time. Maybe I can get rid of some of this wanderlust Pa fusses about." Then looking at Dagan, Jubal spoke again, "Kawliga says you're colonneh—the raven. He says you know things." Without waiting for a reply Jubal went inside leaving Dagan alone with his thoughts.

Good-byes were said the next morning at first light. Dagan did not miss the lingering look and holding hands between Caleb and Kitty. Shouldering their packs, the group headed off with Kawliga in the lead. Andre had drawn a map of sorts. The group would travel overland to Hillsborough, North Carolina, following a well-used road. Then they'd head slightly west toward Salisbury where they'd obtain canoes and head southeast on the Yadkin River that runs into the Pee Dee River. They'd travel the Pee Dee as far as they could to the South Carolina coast and then make their way south along the coast past Georgetown, then to Charlestown. Once in Charlestown, they'd decide how to proceed on to Port Royal.

"Here's a letter to Francis Marion explaining you're only after Gabe and not snooping for the British. If trouble arises, show it. It might come in handy."

"What makes you think he'll help even if we need him?" Caleb had asked.

"Well, we're both French Huguenots," Andre answered, "But more important he rides a horse I gave him. He'll help. If you run into trouble with the colonials in South Carolina, just ask for him."

***

The first part of the journey was easy. Crossing the Cape Fear River, however, had slowed down their journey. It had started to rain the night they'd passed through Hillsborough. The rain continued and by the time they'd got to the river the worn out and drenched men decided to rest before crossing the swollen river.

Kawliga made a lean-to out of pine limbs and brush. This kept most of the rain off the companions and finally a fire was started using, first, pine cones to get a blaze going, and then adding semi-dry wood dug from beneath leaves and pine straw.

The fire popped and crackled and at times there was more smoke than the group would have liked but it did make the little burrow more comfortable. Dagan fixed a pot of coffee and the men made a meal from cold fried chicken and biscuits. As Caleb ate, his mind was more on the cook than the food. Kitty had made the meal the night before they left. It amazed him that she would occupy his thoughts so and he wondered if she thought of him as well.

The group slowly made their way out of their little nest at sun up and after a quick breakfast they built a make-shift raft. Stripping, they piled their belongings on the raft and following Kawliga's example waded into the water. Each holding a rope fastened at the front and back corners of the raft, they made their way across the swollen river.

Once on the other side, they dressed again in wet clothes as the rain had started again. Making their way overland, they were a miserable lot, with each man silent. Dagan continued to worry about Gabe, but did not fail to notice how Kawliga watched over and guided Jubal. His "little shaman." Dagan could sense Jubal had the gift and was glad someone was there to guide the boy, someone who understood.

For two days they marched from sunup to sundown and on the third day they made the little arm of the Yadkin. The rain had been an off and on companion and was now back again.

A makeshift sawmill, a gristmill, and a trading post sat on the banks of the river. A stoop off the side of the sawmill was empty and offered some relief from the rain. Setting down their packs, Dagan could see a rowdy looking group of men sitting on the porch of the trading post, which was just slightly up the hill. The group was a ragged lot. Most had on moccasins or were shoeless. Their britches not much more than dirty tattered rags and their coats had gaping holes. What was visible of their shirts wasn't any better.

"A motley group is it not?" Caleb volunteered.

"Aye," Dagan replied. "I don't like the looks we're getting, but when the rain stops I'm going to see about getting some coffee. That's the only thing we're short on and it might be a long time before we find another trading post."

The sky had darkened with the heavy rain. However, a bolt of lightening lit up the sky so that Dagan could see a sullen man with a battered hat and matted unkempt beard leaning on a porch post, staring at their group.

Kawliga had moved up beside Dagan. "He looking for trouble, maybe want packs," the Indian said. Dagan nodded. That had been his thought as well.

The two groups of men sat staring across the opening at each other. The store sat on higher ground and as the rain fell it made little rivers that made their way down the slope. Areas where the ground was low filled up then the overflow ran on down past the sawmill into the river. The clouds, though dark, were moving fast and soon the thunder and lightening had moved on. The rain slowed to a drizzle and then stopped.

Dagan had just finished a bowl of tobacco and was putting his pipe up when Caleb said, "Here they come." The fragrance of tobacco hung in the air but the musty odour of unwashed bodies became very strong as the group of men approached.

"There's five," Caleb whispered. "One's still on the porch."

"Probably the owner," Dagan replied. "Jubal!"

"Yes, sir."

"I want you to keep your musket ready, and stay slightly over to the side. Make sure we aren't flanked. The rest of us will meet them head on. Follow my signal; we have to have surprise on our side. They'll think because we're outnumbered we'll try to talk."

As the ragged group approached the sullen man said, "Ya'll strangers here about ain't you?"

"We are," Dagan replied.

"Well, we don't take ta strangers," the man said, "Specially Britishers."

The man had closed to within two feet of Dagan by that time. Dagan's action was as swift as a striking snake. Dagan drove the butt of his musket into the man's chest. The force of the impact knocked the breath out of the man's lungs and he cried out as his knees buckled. Before the man hit the ground Dagan brought the barrel of his gun down across the man's head, felling him. When Dagan struck his man, Caleb and Kawliga joined in the battle, Caleb fighting two men. One had been hit so hard his eyes refused to focus, but his partner landed a punch that felt like a lightening bolt had struck Caleb, causing his jaw to pop and immediately ache.

One man had pulled a knife and slashed at Caleb but Kawliga charged him and put the man down with his tomahawk. Caleb wobbled awkwardly for a moment before recovering his wits.

Dagan was facing another of the men who was breathing heavily now. The fight had already lasted longer than he would have thought. Dagan's foe had pulled his blades and the two men circled, each looking for the advantage. Dagan's foot hit a slick muddy spot on the wet ground. Seeing his opponent slip the man slashed out, ripping Dagan's shirt and drawing blood. With the man off balance, Dagan sent a crashing left to the man's face. Blood started to drip from the man's lips and nose as he struggled to keep his feet under him.

At that time, the man who Caleb had first encountered jumped Dagan from behind. Dagan lurched his body trying to loosen the man's grip. The two men struggled and finally they both hit the ground, rolling, wrenching this way and that, before scrambling back on their feet. As Dagan gained his balance, he gave a sudden forward lunge flipping the man over his back and into the rushing river. The man's screams were heard as the swift current swept him downstream. Turning back to the melee, Caleb and Kawliga were holding their own. With three of the rogues down, the numbers were now on Dagan and his group's side.

Kawliga and his opponent circled one another. Kawliga's foe charged and the two hit the wet ground rolling over. Kawliga was much smaller than his man but was quicker. When the man rolled over, he pulled a large wicked knife from his boot. Seeing the blade, Kawliga grabbed a hand full of mud and slung it into the man's face and eyes causing the man to spit and sputter. As the man tried to wipe the mud from his eyes, Kawliga picked up a knife Dagan's foe had dropped and gave it a throw. The blade sunk into the man's throat. With a face full of mud and blood gushing from his neck, the man sunk to his knees then fell face first into the mud Kawliga had just used to his advantage.

Caleb had just landed a blow to his man. It was a vicious left hook. The force of the blow knocked the man backward onto his buttocks. The man felt paralyzed and limp. It suddenly dawned on him the fight was over. His friends were all down. Sitting in the muddy shallows good sense prevailed. The exhausted man used the last of his strength to jump up and run. Kawliga quickly picked up a musket to bring the man down but Dagan intervened.

"Let him go. Let's get up to the post and dry out and maybe get a hot meal."

Jubal had kept his attention on the man on the porch. The man had kept seated all during the fight. As the victors approached the trading post he stood up.

"Glad I am to see 'em gone. Trash. Trash is what they be. Been here three days drinking up my corn squeezing and eating my food without paying a cent. Yes sir, I'm glad to see 'em gone. Supper's on the stove and if you've a mind, a warm bed for the night."

The group was more than willing to accept the man's hospitality.

Chapter Six

The lanthorn hanging off *Warrior's* stern gave a yellow glow through the fog. The lanthorn would swing larboard then starboard with the gentle roll of the flagship. The wet fog bit through the clothes of the men on watch. Like a ghost, patches would drift through sections of the ship making them invisible for a time, then visible again. On the larboard side loomed the rocky shoreline.

"I don't like it," Oxford said as he approached Captain Moffett and Lord Anthony. Both agreed with the master. Above, the faint slapping of cordage against the mast seemed to get on Moffett's nerves.

"Mr Herrod!"

"Aye, Captain."

"Can you not hear that infernal racket?"

"Aye, sir."

"Then dammit, man. Do something about it."

"Aye, sir, right away."

"Good, I hope I don't have to remind you further to take care of your duties."

"No sir, I'll see them done."

Lord Anthony felt clammy as he wiped the moisture from his face. Droplets of moisture had gathered in Oxford's beard and dripped to the deck.

"I can smell the stench of the shore," Oxford sounded distressed. "Not a fit place for a man-o'-war if you ask me."

Anthony had to agree. The Bay of Bundy was narrow and the coast treacherous. Anthony's squadron was escorting a convoy to St. John's, New Brunswick. If Oxford was right the Grand Manan Island was just to larboard.

Privateers had considered this area their personal raiding grounds. It was rumoured they had captured from these waters enough powder and shot to keep Washington's army supplied for a year. Small gunboats would dash in and cut out a supply ship before the convoy escort even knew something was amiss. Anthony had hoped to prevent this from happening to supply ships under his protection. It took daring and experienced captains but Anthony was sure of his captains. Most had been with him for several years. Drakkar was off on independent patrol but Anthony had the rest of his convoy sail in a diamond formation.

Stephen Earl was in temporary command of *Sea Wolf* and sailed at the head of the formation. *Warrior* was further astern of *Sea Wolf*, and *Pigeon* and *Audacity* were on the flanks with Buck bringing up the rear in *Merlin*.

In the middle sailed the convoy. Anthony had held a meeting with all the convoy's captains and laid out specific instructions and sailing plans for the rest of their journey to St. Johns. From Maine, most had already at some point been witness to the raiders and therefore were willing to comply with the Admiral's orders.

Anthony had been looking towards the invisible coast, sensing the nearby dangers he couldn't see.

"Not a fit day ta my way of thinking, sir."

Anthony had been so engrossed with the dangerous coast he'd not been aware Bart had approached. "I think it's a prime day for privateers," Anthony responded. "They could be on us before we know it with this damn fog."

"Aye," Bart answered. "I brung yew a cloth to wipe yer face. Maybe yer glass when the fog lifts."

Looking at his thoughtful cox'n, Anthony asked, "You getting a case of nerves?"

"Nerves? Nay, My Lord, it's a belly full of Silas and that damn ape I'm getting. Do you know, My Lord, Silas asked me to take the damn ape to the head so's he could shat. Damned if I will."

Anthony couldn't help but smile to himself. Bart's anger was more to do with Mr Jewells downing a tankard of rum Bart had made the mistake of setting down on the table while he opened a stern window.

"Think the little bastard can swim?" Bart had asked angrily. "I feel like drowning the bugger."

It was the first time Anthony had ever heard Bart and Silas have words. "You shouldn't a' left it to tempt him," Silas had flung back at Bart. "He doesn't know any better."

"I'll be glad when Caleb gets back and gets his damn ape," Bart had said in a raised voice as he'd stormed out of the pantry.

Well, Anthony thought, *I'll be glad too, more so if Gabe is with him.*

A slight breeze stirred, and then the wind picked up from the south. It rolled back the fog and only small patches remained, and then the remnants thinned and disappeared.

"Gunboats, gunboats to the larboard," the lookout called down.

"Luck," Bart said. "Iffen the wind had held they'd been among us afore we knowed it."

Moffett was quick. He'd already given the order to beat to quarters; however, Earl on *SeaWolf* had already picked out targets and was firing.

The raiders were using galleys, not unlike those the Spanish or Algerians used. The boats carried two short masts and lateen sails with a minimum of canvas and cordage so they could be easily handled by untrained men. They were also pierced for sweeps that gave an added benefit for manoeuvrability. Each gunboat carried two great guns, one in the bow and one in the stern. Each could be elevated, lowered, or transversed. Most of the guns were thirty-two pounders, some even carried several swivels. Even though the vessels looked clumsy, they handled easily enough and each carried ninety to one hundred men. More when needed for a cutting out expedition, such as in the close quarters as the Bay of Bundy.

Upon the sighting, Bart had rushed down and got Lord Anthony's weapons. "Here's your sword and pistol," he said. "Looks like we's in for a bit o' 'citment."

"A hot bit it appears," Anthony replied as one of the gun boats thirty-two pounders cut loose at close range. "*Pigeon* and *Audacity* will never stand up to that. Captain Moffett!"

"Aye, My Lord."

"How many gun boats are attacking?"

"The lookout has made out six, My Lord. Two forward, two astern and just forward of *Merlin*, and two abeam. They're low in the water making our gunnery difficult."

"A hit by gawd," this from the masthead lookout.

"Two to one the gunner laid that himself," Moffett exclaimed.

A sudden explosion and *Warrior* seemed to shudder. Aft a large section of the taffrail had a huge gouge where the thirty-two pound ball had torn its ugly path.

"Luckily, no one was injured. He fired at extreme elevation," Moffett said. "He'd have done better shooting at the rudder instead of the mast."

"Don't give the buggers no ideas," Bart cried.

"One's twixt *SeaWolf* and the convoy," the lookout cried down.

"Mr Herrod?"

"Aye, Cap'n."

"See if we can get a shot with the bowchaser."

"Directly, sir."

"Mr Foxxe, Mr Foxxe to the bow," Herrod called the gunner as he made his way forward.

"Look," Anthony cried, "Looks like *Merlin* has a hit."

"Aye, Mr Buck's done for that bugger, he has," Bart said as he turned toward Anthony. "'Hit don't seem right, do it sir, us uns being bystanders and the like."

"Got a touch of battle lust do you, Bart?"

"Aye, sir, guess I does. It's hard to be a sightseer."

"Don't fret my friend, you'll get your chance and with this fog and smoke it may be sooner than you think."

"My Lord!"

"Yes, Captain."

"Foxxe hit the gunboat but they boarded the supply ship and have cut her out to starboard. *Audacity* has taken chase."

"Very well, Captain, by my count we've sunk three of the raiders. Where are the other three?"

"I'm not sure, My Lord, between the fog of war and nature's fog, visibility is poor. The master swears he can hear the waves on the rocks to larboard so he's edgy."

"Well, I'd like to not get any closer myself," Anthony said. "No telling what else they've got waiting on us."

Moffett's fog of war was the gun smoke. The raiders' thirty-two pounders gave off a tremendous amount of smoke. The heavy smell filling the air and burning one's eyes.

"Deck there, *Pigeon's* grappled with one of the raiders."

"Damme," Moffett shouted. "Can you see the other raider?"

"No sir," the lookout called down.

"Should we send *Merlin* to assist, My Lord?" Moffett asked.

"No, not without knowing where the other raider has gotten. The gunboat will not likely be able to traverse its cannons before it has to repel boarders. Let's just hope Mr Kerry has his wits about him today."

While visibility was difficult, the din of battle was clearly heard between *Pigeon* and the raider. Musket shots, men's cries of anger turned into cries of pain. At moments the gleam of metal could be seen as a blade flashed through the air only to rise bloody.

"Captain Moffett? As we are almost on *Pigeon* send a couple of boats to assist Lieutenant Kerry. I'm sure Captain Dunlap would be more then willing to contribute a squad of marines."

"Aye, My Lord, I'll see to it."

Looking down from his flagship, Anthony could see the dirty chop of a wave against the hull. Mangled bodies and debris was all about, some of it thumping again and again against *Warrior* as she moved slowly ahead. The battle was all but over but he received no pleasure. How many American and British lives had been lost? It seemed different when he had been in the thick of battle but now...now! Bart was right, being a sightseer was difficult.

"Captain's compliments, sir, but *Merlin* has signalled they've cut off escape by the raiders and *Audacity* has boarded and retook the ship."

"Thank you, Mr Dewy. Any word on the other raiders?"

"No sir, but we're still searching. The master thinks they took wind."

"Well, we'll see if the master is right."

"Aye, My Lord."

"Looks like they've took the other bugger sir, they've put up a flag," Bart volunteered. "Brave man that Mister Kerry is, not the smartest block I've known, but he ain't no coward, sir."

"Bart."

"Aye, sir."

"You're talking about a King's officer."

"He won't be long, sir, iffen you don't teach 'em some smarts. Likely get himself and half his crew kilt. 'Scretion is what 'e needs ta learn."

"You mean discretion."

"Aye, sir, 'scretion and plenty of it, I'm thinking."

Chapter Seven

Skirting the usual wagon path, Lum worked his way toward the slaves' quarters that sat scattered among the oak trees behind the main house. A haggard looking outbuilding had started to lean and was in danger of falling. This building sat in such a way that it blocked the view of Lum's small cabin from the rear windows and back porch of the main house.

It was here that Lum halted the mule. "Whoa… Whoa now Bessie." As soon as the wagon stopped the mule immediately started cropping grass and swishing flies with her tail. Helping Nanny down the two slaves went to the back of the wagon to help with Gabe.

"You don't think we can take him up to the house?" Faith asked.

"Child, you see dat uniform. Dis man is one o' dem heathen Britishers like tried to take Charlestown. Maybe he even was a part of it," Nanny said rebuking the girl. "Master Adam see this man he'll put him in jail like he does with folks at times. Shucks, he might even jus shoot him."

Hearing this stopped Faith's objections. Nanny was right.

"What you ought to be worrying about is what's gonna happen to Lum if the marse finds dat man heah. Like as not he'll set Marse Hindley loose on Lum with dat whip o' his."

"I won't let him," Faith said trying to be stern.

"Not much you can do, child," Lum said for the first time. "We's a chance it. I don't like to see none of God's creatures suffer. Now let's get this po' soul inside and you go fetch Ruby. She's helped with delivering babies and fixing mules and da hosses and such. So maybe she can help him. Besides she'll keep her mouth shut."

***

Several days went by with Gabe suffering from high fevers. Ruby had washed and cleaned his wounds and put several stitches in his leg using a hair from ole Bessie, the mule's tail. Food was sneaked in for Gabe, and Faith was able to get some clothes together so Gabe's uniform could be cleaned and repaired. As Gabe's health improved he became anxious to be up and about. Lying in Lum's bed, he watched the single candle as it gave off a faint yellow glow.

The flickering flame caused wavering shadows on the rough wooden walls of the cabin. The shadows would take shapes that would disappear, and reappear, and then other shapes would merge together. Watching the candles and hearing the slaves whisper among themselves Gabe grew afraid, not of death but of capture.

How long would he be held? He thought of his brother Gil; surely he'd think he was dead. What of Dagan? Gabe was sure he was alive. If he were unhurt he'd be coming to get him. At times Gabe would fall asleep and awaken with Faith sitting next to him usually running her fingers along the gray furrow on his scalp. Once her kissing his lips woke him. When he reached for her she darted out of the cabin.

Damned if this girl didn't intrigue him, Gabe thought. He got to where when he heard her enter the cabin he'd pretend to be asleep just to feel her hands, soft and tender, caressing his face and always touching his gray furrow.

"I know you're not asleep. You're just lying there pretending and hoping for another kiss but you'll not get it."

Listening to Faith caused a slight smile Gabe couldn't prevent. He opened his eyes and looking at the beauty staring down at him said, "God, I'm in love."

"Well, I still ain't kissing you," Faith replied. "Here I done saved yore hide and you playing possum with me to steal a kiss. I ought to turn you in is what I ought to do, and I still might." But as Faith rose from the side of Gabe's bed she looked to see if anyone was watching, quickly leaned over and gave Gabe a quick peck on the lips, then without a word she dashed off.

With his strength returning Gabe would get out of bed and move about the cabin. "Keep away from de doh," Lum had begged. Tonight he could stand it no longer. He had to be about, he had to have some fresh air.

"Well, if you dat determined we'll take a stroll when the marse goes down," Lum said. Gabe could tell the old black man didn't like the idea but also understood Gabe's needs.

Walking through the shadows Gabe paused under a giant oak tree. The front of the house was there before him. It was a huge white house with eight columns. It was set up high off the ground, and while the house was wood, it had been bricked from the ground up to the porch. Gabe counted ten steps that had to be twenty feet wide, leading up to the porch.

"Why is the house built so high?" Gabe asked Lum.

"Cause da' be a flood. This heah's called de low country. Da's a river what flows to the marsh and den da's the ocean. Course back dat a-way's a swamp. Marse Hindley says they's crocogators in dat swamp what eat up people."

Gabe had never heard of a crocogator but didn't pursue it. "Why do they brick up around the house?" Gabe asked, still curious as to the design.

"Why dat helps keep out de rattlers and cottonmouths and copperheads. It's where they stoh the potatoes and vegetables. And when we get eggs from the hen house we keep 'em dere cause it's the coolest place. Marse Adam keeps his wine and cider down dere too."

"What are those buildings off that way towards the river?"

"That's the sawmill then past dat is the gristmill. We can do bout anything heah on Marse Adam's plantation. We's got a blacksmith shop and dat big building over there is de ship's warehouse and jail."

"Ship's warehouse. What's in that?"

"Why thangs dey bring in off ships. We plantation slaves, we don't go over there. Only Marse Hindley's boys go over there. They's men watch over dat place with guns."

"Hmmm," Gabe said deep in thought. Was this where the gunpowder was to be sent after being unloaded from the *Turtle*?

"Afore Missy Faith's mama and daddy died they owned de plantation and Marse Adam shipped de cotton and wood and stuff. But now he head of it all. He is Missy Faith's uncle but she don't care much for him."

"Why is that?" Gabe inquired.

"Well, she don't say, but Nanny says Marse Adam look at her like a woman from town and not his dead brother's child."

"Tell me," Gabe asked, "Why is it you and Nanny are so close to Faith? More so than the other slaves."

Wiping the sweat from his balding scalp with a dirty rag, Lum placed his battered hat back on. "Nanny was Missy's wet nurse and I was Missy's daddy, Mr Thomas Montique's, personal servant. Marse Adam, he jus kinda lets us be, less it pleases him to do utter wise."

"What's that sound?" Gabe asked. A loud baying sound had broken out by the warehouse.

"Something's going on over by de warehouse dats set dem dawgs off. Let's get on outta heah afore trouble starts."

Turning the two found themselves face to face with Hindley, the overseer. He had two other men with him, both carrying muskets.

"Who you got there, Lum?"

"He's jus a friend o' Missy Faith's, suh."

"Missy Faith's friend. Well I ain't never seen him around before."

"Naw, suh, he's a new friend," Lum answered the overseer.

"Does Mister Adam know his niece has a guest?"

"I don't rightly know, suh. I's jus lookin after him foh the missy since he been sickly."

"I see," Hindley said suspiciously, "What are ya'll doing out this late?"

"We just took a notion to stretch our legs."

"Have you stretched your legs over by the warehouse, Lum?"

"Oh naw, suh, we show to gawd ain't, suh. You knows ole Lum ain't going no where's around Marse Adam's warehouse."

"What about him?" Hindley asked pointing to Gabe with a curled black bullwhip in his hand.

"Oh naw suh, naw suh, you know I wouldn't let nobody do dat and me catch de blame for it."

BANG!...BANG!...

"Shots down by the river," one of Hindley's men said.

The bays of the dog continued and added to the noise. Loud voices could be heard.

"Looks like whoever was at the warehouse is trying to escape down by the river, shouldn't we move on?" Hindley knew his man was right but something smelled about this man with Lum.

Now lights were on at the big house and Adam Montique's voice could be heard. "What's all the commotion?"

Making a quick decision Hindley ordered, "Smith, you and Lum take this man on up to Mister Montique while Ledbetter and I go see what's about down by the river."

Gabe had the desire to run but knew if he did he'd have little chance of making it. He also knew things would go worse for Lum and he didn't want to endanger the old slave. As the three men approached the mansion's front steps Gabe saw a man standing up on the porch.

"Well, I'll be damned," he thought. He'd known there was something familiar about the name Montique but couldn't place it. Now he knew. This was the man from Antigua. He had owned the house Commodore Gardner had lived in. He'd also had numerous ships under contract to the Royal Navy. Now it appeared he had chosen to fight with the colonials. I wonder if he still has Royal Navy contracts, Gabe thought to himself. Stepping to the edge of the porch, Montique held a lanthorn up high.

"What do we have here?" he asked Smith.

"Some white man with Lum. Mr Hindley says to fetch him to you as he claims to be a friend of Miss Faith's.

"Well, step forward," Montique ordered. Holding up the lanthorn he noted the worn clothes Gabe had on. As Gabe reached the top step he decided to act the part of an old acquaintance.

"We've met sir," he said. "I had the pleasure of being introduced to you at a reception given by Commodore Gardner in Antigua." Gabe held out his hand to Montique whose face became hard, and twisted into a glare, his eyes like burning coals as the flame from the lanthorn reflected in them.

With clinched teeth, Montique spat on the porch. "Damned if we haven't. Mr Smith, we have before us the bastard son of a British Admiral."

Without thinking Gabe lunged at Montique but before he could reach him Smith clubbed him with the butt of his musket. As Gabe went down he heard a woman screaming, "Uncle, what have you done?"

Chapter Eight

Once on the river travel was much faster. The old store owner was so grateful to Dagan and his group for running off the "river trash" that he sent a runner to a nearby Indian village to set up a barter. After a short time, Kawliga had made a trade for two canoes.

"They're not in their prime," Caleb said of the canoes, "But for a sack each of tobacco, flour, and salt I think we did better than we hoped for."

It sure beats walking, Dagan thought. He'd always felt more comfortable on water than on land. They travelled for several days on the river, at times they'd have to haul the canoes overland for a short distance in an effort to miss rocky rapids, snags, or fallen trees. Then once past the hazards, the journey downstream would begin anew.

Each night they'd make camp on shore and far enough from the river their fire couldn't be easily seen.

"Still smell smoke, but no see blaze," Kawliga had said in his short sentences. Kawliga had also proved to be an excellent cook. He fried bacon at night, cooking enough to have for breakfast in the morning without cooking again. He was good at cooking fried cornbread in the bacon grease and on a couple nights he even fried sliced sweet potatoes. Jubal seemed to think nothing of Kawliga's cooking abilities, but Caleb and Dagan were impressed.

"Sure beats the hell out of old Frosty's cooking," Caleb swore.

"That it does," Dagan agreed but both men missed the old coot.

One morning Kawliga spoke to Jubal who in turn turned to Dagan. Motioning his head toward the Indian, Jubal said, "He thinks we're in South Carolina now."

"How can he tell?" Caleb asked.

"Lots of ways," Jubal replied. "There's more moss on the tree limbs that are hanging over the river. The lands more flat, more swamp and backwater. You don't see the clearly defined river banks we've been used to."

The air that had smelled like honeysuckle now seemed to have a fetid odour. Birds stood in the shallows. A white wood ibis on the bank beat its wings and lifted off. A sound like a bellow was heard.

As the bird lifted off Kawliga pointed. "Alligator scare bird, make it fly."

Lily pads were thick in areas, some with bright yellow blossoms. Turtles sunning on logs made plopping sounds as they slid into the water as the canoes passed by. Herons stood high on their long thin yellow legs.

These were all changes Dagan and Caleb had seen but had not realized the significance. They were out of their element and Dagan was once again thankful he'd been able to obtain such guides as Kawliga and Jubal.

"The only things I've seen different," Caleb responded, "is more mosquitoes and snakes."

That night it rained again and the men slept under the boats. They had turned the boats over and using downed tree limbs to prop them up, creating a shelter of sorts that kept things dryer and made the night more comfortable.

"Supplies are about out so we have to get some soon," Dagan told the party that night before they turned in. "If we don't find a trading place on the river soon we'll have to go inland before we continue to Charlestown."

Rising early the following morning the group rowed with a determination, putting a great distance behind them before the sun started to set. It was like they could all feel the urgency that possessed Dagan's very soul. As the canoes turned toward the shore another bird caught Caleb's eye, "Look at that. That's the prettiest bird I ever seen."

As the colourful bird flew off, Jubal said, "That's a bunting."

"*I'm not sure what it is,*" Caleb thought to himself. "*But I wouldn't mind seeing Kitty with a thin nightgown on the same green colour as the bird's feathers had been.*" Caleb was still enjoying his thoughts when the canoe made a grinding sound in the mud. With his mind thus distracted he jumped from the canoe to pull it up on shore.

As soon as he landed he felt something move beneath his feet then felt a sharp pain in his leg. A blur went past Caleb's eyes then he saw Kawliga's tomahawk embedded in the ground in front of the canoe. A headless snake lay writhing and flopping in coils.

"Let's see the bite," Kawliga said as he laid Caleb flat and using his knife cut the lacings on Caleb's moccasins and then split his trouser leg. A red whelp was present and one small dot of blood. Not two dots, but one. Jubal wiped the spot of blood away.

"Not deep, just enough to draw blood and looks like only one fang."

Kawliga walked back over to where the dead snake lay. A large bulge was around the snake's middle. The Indian slit open the snake and a rat fell to the ground. "Snake not long eat, broke fang. Snake slow with full belly. Caleb get sick maybe, not likely die."

Kawliga then walked a few steps to a plant. "See plant, snake root. You chew root you not die," he said as he dug up the root. "You chew."

"I'm damn glad to know your expert opinion," Caleb said, trying not to show the pain he was feeling from his throbbing leg and also trying not to gag on the root he chewed.

Jubal broke into a laugh, "Look here, this canebrake had thirteen rattles. That's the same number of colonies we got. You've done been bit by a colonial rattlesnake Caleb." Dagan burst out laughing and in spite of his pain, so did Caleb.

***

Kawliga's prophecy proved true. Caleb lived but his leg did swell and was very sore as the group made their way down the long stretch of wharfs after finally reaching Charlestown.

"Damme," Dagan said, "place looks like a floating market."

Bay Street was lined with wholesale stores and residences that ran parallel to the Cooper River. The river was choked with brigantines, sloops, and schooners

from abroad. Tied-up as they were, there was little hope
of escaping any enterprising British naval patrol. From
upriver, barges, dugouts, and canoes made their way
down from the interior, full of country produce to be
sold to the town folks.

Negro slaves were everywhere. A few Cherokee
Indians were also about so no one paid much attention
to Kawliga.

"Look!" Caleb tapped Dagan and pointed to a man
holding a sign: *Mary McDowell's most notorious brothel for
lewd women - Pinckney Street.*

"What's a brothel?" Jubal asked.

Both Caleb and Dagan turned and stared at the
boy. For once, both were speechless. "Your Pa will tell
you about it," Dagan finally managed to say.

"Why can't you?"

"Well, some things need to be discussed between a
father and son."

"But Pa ain't here."

"You'll see him soon enough."

"You just don't want to tell me. Well, I reckon I'll
just go over to Pinckney Street and find out."

"Humm…" Caleb said, "Might not be too bad an
idea."

"Shut up Caleb," Dagan said, then turned to Jubal,
"You ever read the Bible?"

But before he could explain further, Jubal cried out,
"Mr Francis…Mr Francis over here."

Dagan was both relieved and concerned. Relieved
he didn't have to explain what a brothel was but
concerned about meeting the enemy. He had the letter
of introduction but had hoped he wouldn't need it. Now
he was facing Francis Marion, a colonial colonel.

Marion was a smallish man. He wore a crimson jacket and a battered helmet with a silver crescent and the words "liberty or death" was on his head. He had a slight limp. Seeing the limp was noticed, Marion said by way of explanation, "Broke my ankle during the battle of Fort Moultrie."

"I see," Dagan said trying to decide how to proceed with this man who could have him thrown in prison, or worse...shot. After a second Dagan decided to be truthful and straightforward. "Colonel, I'm a British sailor. I'm looking for my nephew who commands a British warship. I have a letter for you from my uncle, Andre, Jubal's father whom I believe you know well."

Without the slightest change in his facial expression and demeanour, Marion said, "Well, it appears we have a bit to discuss. Let's move to a place more suitable than the Bay Street wharf. I know of a nice little tavern that puts together a fantastic Frogmore stew. Shall we go?"

Dagan had no knowledge of what Frogmore stew was but felt compelled to follow the man known as the Swamp Fox as he limped off toward the tavern.

***

Marion read Andre's letter and listened to Dagan's story. Then he said, "I'll get you to Beaufort...if I have your word you'll collect your nephew and be off. No spying, no sabotage, just get your kin and get."

"You have my word," Dagan replied solemnly. "We will protect ourselves if we have to but otherwise we'll avoid trouble when we can."

"Fair enough," Marion stated, "Wait here till you hear from my messenger."

In less than an hour, a man approached Dagan's group as they sat around a table at the tavern where Marion had left them. He was dressed in buckskin britches, a homespun Woolsey shirt and an ill-fitting crimson jacket that bore a silver crescent, the mark of South Carolina's second regiment.

In a low voice the man spoke, "You the Britishers?"

When Dagan nodded his answer the man said, "Colonel Marion sent me to guide you to fetch your kin and keep you outta trouble whilst we's about it. Name's Rud."

"How shall we travel?" Dagan inquired.

"It'd be quicker to take a boat," the man said, "But that'd attract more attention to us so's we'll go overland but stay off the main road. The colonel gave me a pass in case we get stopped and questioned. But, he reckons it best we try to avoid any sojers if possible."

"How long will it take?" Dagan asked as the rest of the group remained silent.

"'Pends on if you can keep up," Rud answered. He had noted Caleb favouring his leg. "Day, maybe two."

Finishing his tankard of ale, Caleb stood and stepped around the table. "When can we leave?" he asked.

"Quick as you get your plunder together," Rud replied, "There's still enough light left we can make our way outta the city and have a good jump on the morrow."

Chapter Nine

Someone was screaming. Screams intermingled with cries and loud sobs. As Gabe tried to clear the fog from his brain he could hear the cries. They were muffled but close by, women—the cries were women—and seemed to be coming beyond the wall where Gabe had been lying. As he reached to touch the back of his head he felt a weight tugging at his arms. He was manacled. A chain went from wrist to wrist, then another was around his waist and still another attached the chains shackling his arms to the one around his waist. The chain around his waist had a tail and was attached to something. It was dark in his prison so Gabe on his knees followed the length of chain to a wall. About three feet off the hardwood floor he found the chain was attached to a large ring bolt. Not unlike that on a slaver they'd taken as a prize last year.

Next to the wall the sounds from the next room were much clearer. Now there was a mixture of sounds. In addition to the cries and whimpers of women there was also the laugh of men. Right away he recognized the voice of Montique and Hindley. Hindley was addressing his boss.

"Can the men have a turn now, Mr Montique?"

A slight pause then Montique answered, "Tomorrow night, but tell that bull Smith if I lose another from his sodomizing he'll pay. The Dey of

Algiers doesn't take it kindly when his merchandise can't hold their bowels."

"I'll warn him, sir. I'll threaten to take the cost of the wench from his pay."

"And I'll have the hide off his back as well," Montique said.

As the two men stepped out of the prison where the captive women were kept, Montique could see Faith sitting on the top step of the plantation house. She had her legs drawn up to her chest with her chin on her knees.

"Has she come around yet?" Hindley inquired.

"No, not yet, and I'm losing patience," Montique answered. "If she's not willing by the time I return from Charlestown I may send her on a trip to Algiers. I could get more for her than the whole group we got penned up."

"Should I help persuade her some?" Hindley asked, hoping to have his way with Faith. He'd seen her in the low cut dresses acting so innocent. He'd also seen her naked. He had climbed the oak tree and lain on a limb while Nanny readied the tub and Faith undressed as he watched. She was ripe and he was ready to pick the fruit.

Montique had come to a stop and appeared to be considering Hindley's suggestion, "No, not yet. Keep an eye on her. Give her free rein, but watch her closely. If she doesn't want me when I get back, Ali Dey can have her. Let's see how she likes the Dey's 'keeper of the honey' watching over her night and day. The big eunuch stands with his arms crossed and a great scimitar in his hand guarding the only entrance to the harem's quarters."

Montique seemed to be thinking aloud as he continued speaking, "A beautiful blonde is worth a lot, but a beautiful blonde virgin is priceless." Shaking his head, Montique appeared to have made up his mind. "No, don't touch her Hindley…keep your eye on her, but don't touch her." These last words were filled with menace.

As they parted in different directions, a drizzle started, then the rain came harder. *Damn*, thought Montique, *it will be a slow muddy trip to Charlestown.*

***

Gabe awoke with a start. In spite of the cool damp air he was sweating. He had been dreaming of the explosion on *Turtle*. The sudden blast that sent him cartwheeling into the air as the vessel became a roaring inferno. High through the air Gabe had been hurled, still clutching the *Turtle's* captain. The air burned his lungs as sheets of flames seemed to reach out for him. At some point he turned loose of the burning corpse that seconds before had been a man. Then down, down he plunged into the muddy darkness of the trough where the remains of *Turtle* filled the sky with fiery orange debris.

Gabe wiped his face with a grubby sleeve. He smelled the marsh. He could not yet see about him so it was still early but he knew his prison was close to the marsh. He could smell it and it brought back memories of his childhood. His father would take him hunting wildfowl on the marshes that lay along the Thames. It was one of the few times Father had seemed completely relaxed. He was just Father on the hunting trips, not Admiral Lord James Anthony. It had been the two of them…Dagan, and his father's servant.

Memories…A shackled prisoner…would he live long enough to have further memories? He would like to have a life full of memories built around Faith. He suddenly realized he was deeply in love. He'd like to share life with Faith. She could bear him a son and he could take his son hunting in the marshes as his own father had done.

***

"Shh…," Rud held his fingers to his lips. The group of men was in a thicket just off the main road. Limbs from the great oaks hung low; some even touched the ground. Moss hung from the limbs and old acorns crunched under their feet as they made their way as silently as possible.

At Rud's warning, they had squatted down to be even less visible. A coach was approaching on the road. The sound of the horses' hooves on the road was clearer and then rounding a slight bend, the coach was visible. Two men sat on top, a driver and a servant both dressed in red livery. As the coach passed a great crest emblazoned on the door and, with the window shade up, a man could be seen.

"Montique," Dagan hissed, "I knew it would be him."

"That's the devil himself is it?" Rud asked.

"Aye, that's him. Well, maybe things will go better with him away."

***

Light flooded the room as the door was opened. Two men stepped in, one with a musket and one with a plate of food and a cup of water.

"You's hungry?" the man carrying the food asked as he set it down on the floor. "I don't know why we bother to feed ye anyhow. You're a dead man soon as Mr Montique returns."

"Mister Montique say iffen he see's Captain Crawford he's gonna tell him he's got the man what took 'is ship and got his young un in a British jail. It could be Captain Crawford might pay to put his hand on ye. Might use ye to barter foh his kid or he might jus kill you his own self."

Then laughing the two turned to leave. Wanting to get a better look at his surroundings Gabe called out, "I have to go."

"What?" the man with the musket called.

"I have to go," Gabe repeated. "Nature calls."

"Well shit in your pants then sit in it," the other man replied cruelly.

"If I do I'm sure it will be you who has to clean up after I'm dead."

The man holding the rifle snickered, his rotten teeth showing. "He's right, Luther. Smith will sure put you to cleaning up the mess."

"Ah right! Hold that gun on him and if he so much as flinches you part his hair with a bullet right where that gray streak be."

Outside Gabe could see he was being kept in a warehouse that indeed was almost at the river's edge. He could see a boardwalk and what appeared to be a dock. That was probably where stolen goods were brought in and out. Attached to the side of the warehouse was a smaller building. Bars filled the windows and young women peered out as he passed. Luther saw him looking and snatched on his chain causing Gabe to stumble.

Laughing at Gabe, Luther said, "Lookers ain't they? To bad you can't have any but if you beg I'll ask Smith if he'll let you watch as we has our pleasure. That will be just afore Mr Montique takes his pleasure in killin you."

Look as he may Gabe could find nothing that would aid in his escape. He'd hoped to get a glimpse of Faith but that was not to be. Once back in the warehouse the sun was starting to shine through high windows and cracks between the wall boards. The warehouse was full. Barrels labelled rum were stacked against the rear wall to one side and several cannons filled the other side.

Boxes labelled muskets were stacked as high as a man's head. There were also boxes labelled shoes, shirts, blankets, and britches. Powder kegs were stacked, more boxes labelled bullets, buckshot, nails, and one small box labelled stockings. Sail canvas was stacked, and down the middle, ship's spars were stored.

Turning, Gabe focused on top of the barrel next to him, a lanthorn. Luther had been careless and left the lanthorn he'd used to see with when he unlocked Gabe's chain. It was sitting on a barrel. It was no longer lit but it was there. If he couldn't escape Gabe thought at least he might be able to light the lanthorn and destroy the warehouse. At least he'd die with the knowledge Montique wouldn't be able to use his ill-gotten goods.

Gabe slumped down against the wall feeling the rough wall scratch at his back as he did so. The pain suddenly made him feel desolate. In his despair he hung his head. *Dagan, where are you? Gil, Faith, Dagan.* They all filled his mind and for the first time in a long time Gabe found himself reciting the Lord's Prayer.

***

Rud, Dagan, and the group arrived at the plantation just before dusk, skirting their way through an oak thicket trying to keep out of everyone's sight including the slaves. As they stopped at the last line of oaks before a large clearing they were able to take in most of the plantation. A row of shotgun houses built close together was obviously the slave quarters.

The glow of candles was noted in a few open windows. It was easy to pick out the stables; a foundry indicated the blacksmith shop and another outbuilding looked like a sawmill. As darkness overtook the dusk the woods seem to come alive. Lightening bugs flashed their momentary glow, and mosquitoes buzzed about. It seemed all the insects decided to sing at once.

Next to the slave quarters a loud shout sounded and then a dog howled mournfully, followed by half a dozen more dogs starting to howl. At this point, someone stamped hard on the porch and another shout, and then a sudden yelp and the dogs were quiet.

"Smell the marsh?" Jubal asked.

"Aye lad, you couldn't miss it," Dagan answered.

"Look there," Rud was pointing to a large building. One man was holding a lanthorn in one hand and a gun in the other. Another man was unlocking a door.

Dagan suddenly rose from where he had been crouching and took a half step out of the shadows. "Gabe is there," he spoke to no one in particular.

Kawliga moved up next to Dagan. "Man there, colonneh?"

"Aye," Dagan answered and turned back toward the thicket only to come to a dead stop as Kawliga whispered, "Women too."

"Women?" Dagan was surprised and turned back toward the buildings. Sure enough, after listening closely voices were heard and then in the lamplight a woman appeared looking out between the bars of the jail. Then gazing further he could see a woman and a black man, probably a slave, coming down the steps of the plantation house. Stepping back into the thicket, he passed on his and Kawliga's findings.

"Rud, I gave my word to Colonel Marion not to spy and only protect myself as needed. Now it looks like it's time for a bit of action. I came to get Gabe, but it looks like Montique is more than a pirate. It appears he's a slaver as well, black and white. If you wish to go back now give my respects to the colonel. If you stay...well things could get bloody."

Without hesitating Rud answered, "I'll stay. I don't like no white women being mistreated."

"Good enough," Dagan said but mentally decided to keep Caleb close by. He knew his metal. "Jubal!"

"Yes sir."

"I want you and Kawliga to go back and skirt around the edge of the clearing and see if those boards yonder by the big building lead to a dock or a boat. If there is a boat large enough for all of us and several women take control of it. If not work your way back and stop us before we head down the boardwalk. Don't take chances. Understand...don't take any chances."

Looking at Kawliga, the Indian nodded then the two were off. Dagan then asked Caleb, "You ready?"

"As ever."

"The leg?"

"It's fine, lets be at it."

Turning to Rud, Dagan placed his hands on the man's shoulder. "You're the woodsman, lead on."

***

Gabe was not sure why, but he felt better. He'd drifted off to sleep after his prayer and awoke at the rattle of chains at the door. Luther and rotten teeth were back. "Eat your grub and in an hour or so you can listen as we has ourselves a shindig. Smith will have the women squealing like pigs. You can't have no cunny but you can listen."

Gabe ate the offered stew and biscuit and was quite surprised at how good it was. Whoever the cook was knew their way around a stove. About the time Gabe finished he heard voices outside arguing.

One was Luther's, the other a female...Faith, it was Faith. Then the arguing came to a halt and the door opened. Luther spoke once more, "Mr Hindley's gone and you know it, but soon as he gets back we's gonna fetch him. You know Mr Montique don't allow you down here where the prisoners are." Then he pushed the door shut and left.

He had the keys to the chain locks so there was no chance in the man escaping. Therefore, he let Faith have her way. He knew it wasn't right but he wasn't about to physically stop her, not yet he wasn't. Not that he hadn't dreamed of touching her, but unless Hindley said to, he wouldn't touch a hair on her head, no sir, nary a hair.

Once in the warehouse, Lum handed the lanthorn to Faith and sat down in the shadows of the opposite corner away from Gabe and Faith. *They shouldn't be here at all but with him along maybe Hindley's white trash guards would think twice before touching the girl,* Lum thought.

Faith lifted the lanthorn and as she did Gabe stood up. Seeing Gabe, Faith rushed to him setting the lanthorn on top of a barrel that was close by.

"Oh Gabe, I was so afraid they'd hurt you. My uncle, how could he do such evil things? Oh Gabe."

Gabe could smell Faith's fresh-washed hair, the faint scent of her perfume, the woman smell. After the damp musty odour of the warehouse it was like heaven. He reached for her and she came to him. This time she kissed him long and hard, not like the sudden fleeting pecks she'd given when he'd been laid up in Lum's cabin. She crushed her body into Gabe's, kissing, hugging, and weeping all at the same time. He could feel her breast, her heartbeat, the smoothness of her skin.

After a long breath, she broke away and gasped, "I love you. God, Gabe, I don't know when or how, but I love you. I've got to get you out of here. I'll confront Uncle Adam and if he doesn't turn you loose I'll go get help."

How naïve, Gabe thought. *How young, innocent and naïve.* All his loneliness was forgotten with just her kiss. "I love you too," he stammered, "I want you…I want you to be my wife."

"Gabe, oh Gabe, God yes, let's get you out of here now."

"Hold on to ye horse now, missy."

"Hindley!"

"At your service, madam."

"Turn him loose."

"Afraid I can't missy. The master seems to have his sights set on a special death for that un. A painful, drawn-out death, I'm bettin. However, if you was to be kindly I could put it to him so as he'd die right away. That way they'd be no suffering. Say he was trying to escape."

"Go to hell, Hindley."

"What! The she-cat is snarling a bit is she?" Then Hindley sneered, "Lets see if you can do anything but snarl."

Reaching out he grasped her top and fiercely ripped it away, exposing her breasts. Gabe lunged at the man but the chains brought him up short. Grabbing a length of trace chain, Hindley swung at Gabe. The chains cut a gash along his cheek. Faith kicked Hindley, who whirled and grabbed Faith bodily and hurled her to the floor.

As Gabe reached out attempting to help again, Hindley kicked him savagely in the stomach before turning his attention back to Faith. The urge to jump up on her feet and run was almost overpowering, but Faith couldn't leave Gabe. Hindley would surely kill him.

"Uncle Adam will have your back flayed for this you bastard," Faith spat at her tormentor.

"He will surely try, she-cat, so I better enjoy what I can before he returns." Hindley then took a step toward

Faith and she slapped him. Enraged, he snatched her to him and gave a ringing slap to her face.

"What you need, little she-cat, is a taming, and I aim to give it to you starting now." Hindley then forced Faith back and down over a wooden table. His fingers dug into her soft breasts, bruising them as he did so. He tore at her skirt and pulled it up over her knees, enjoying the feel of the soft flesh of her upper thighs.

"Get off me," Faith screamed as she loosened a hand and clawed at her attacker's face as he thrust toward her.

From the shadow a large black man arose. "Leave her be, Mr Hindley."

"Get out," Hindley shouted.

"I said leave her be," Lum repeated and this time he grasped Hindley's shoulder.

Furious and half crazy over the whole affair, Hindley jumped up and hit Lum with a strong blow to the head. "I said get out nigger."

Turning his attention back to Faith, he slapped her again as he flung her back down on the table and thrust at her once again. Out of nowhere Hindley felt himself being snatched around as an axe was plunged deep into his skull. He never heard the scream he let out as he slumped to the floor, but Luther and Rotten Teeth did.

Lum was helping Faith to her feet and trying to cover her nakedness when the door burst open.

"Well looky heah…looks like the nigger done killed Mr Hindley and is raping Miss Faith. What you thank?" Luther asked his partner.

"Kill us a nigger and taste a bit o' sweet nectar all in one night. Course we'll have to kill missy too, but that's after we licked all the honey outta the pot."

"You're not killing anyone, my friend." Dagan, Caleb, and Rud had walked up on the two without being heard, so intent had they been staring at the partially clad Faith.

"Who'er you?"

"Does it matter," Dagan asked.

"Sho nuff does," Rotten Teeth spoke. "Luther, he ain't even got a gun."

"Then kill him," Luther cried.

As he did, Dagan stepped aside. Luther and Rotten Teeth saw Caleb and Rud too late. Caleb shot Luther in the chest with his pistol. Holding his musket casually, without aiming Rud fired, his ball hitting Rotten Teeth in the stomach taking a button from his shirt and pushing it through his backbone.

Gabe tried to rise, Faith and Dagan both rushed to him. "Still getting yourself into a fix," Dagan said sarcastically, but feeling an immense sense of relief.

Gabe stood with help, tried to smile as he said, "Aye, but she's worth it." Then directing his attention to Caleb, Gabe continued, "The man you shot keeps the keys to the locks in his coat pocket."

Finding the keys, Gabe was soon released and Rud went to set the imprisoned girls free. Turning to Faith, Dagan asked, "How long before we have company?"

"I'm not sure," Faith replied. "My uncle went to meet some men in Charlestown this morning so I don't expect him back till tomorrow or the next day. However, usually when he returns from his trips he brings several men with him, but I think we're safe enough for now."

Looking at Faith, who was still not completely covered, an uncomfortable Dagan asked further, "And your uncle is?"

"Adam Montique."

"I knew it," Dagan said. "The man has been plotting against us from the start."

"Aye," Gabe replied. "He thought I was out after his man slugged me but I came to in time to hear him brag about how he was the brains behind the pirates we faced in the West Indies. He killed most of his captives, but the women, especially the blond women, he sold to the Dey of Algiers. The others he took his pleasures with, and then turned them over to Hindley and his men."

Caleb, who had gone to check on Jubal and Kawliga, returned and reported their findings. "There's a boat right enough. Kawliga surprised the man on board and he's trussed up properly now."

"How big is the boat?" Gabe asked.

"It ought to hold us all. The tide appears to be on the ebb though so we need to hurry."

"Well, get the women to the boat. Then look around and get us some weapons, food, and water."

When Caleb had departed, Gabe turned to Dagan, "This place has enough supplies in it to keep an army going for months. We'll lay a charge and on our way out we'll light a fuse and finish the job we started."

Gabe had his back to Faith and so he could not see her hand go to her mouth and the pallor that crept across her face.

"No!" Dagan said.

"Did you say no," Gabe asked, not believing his ears.

"I gave my word to Colonel Marion I'd fetch you and protect myself but I'd do no more mischief," Dagan explained.

"But these supplies, this man cared nothing for the war. He's filling his pockets at both countries' expense."

"I gave my word, Gabe, same as you did to the smuggler that time."

Gabe gave a sigh and turned to Faith, "Lets get your things together."

"I...can't Gabe, I can't go with you."

"But we're to be married. You said you'd marry me."

"I can't Gabe."

"Don't you love me, Faith?"

"Yes, yes with all my heart."

"Then let's get some things and go."

"I told you I can't Gabe."

"Why?"

"Cause you're the enemy...our countries are at war...Maybe after the war, Gabe, but not now. We believe in different causes."

"You can't stay here, Faith, your uncle, what will he do when he returns?"

Looking very determined Faith said, "Live Oak is mine. My father made this place what it is and I intend to keep it. My father had influential friends in Savannah. I will go there. They will help me, I'm sure. Nanny and Uncle Lum..." Faith stopped in mid-sentence. "Take Uncle Lum with you Gabe."

"But missy," Lum broke in.

"No, you can't stay. You killed a white man and they'd hang you for sure. It wouldn't matter why you did it. Sooner or later they'd get you alone and string you up."

"My place is with you, Miss Faith," Lum pleaded.

With tears in her eyes, Faith placed her hands on Lum's face and kissed his cheek. "You've always watched out for me ain't you, Uncle Lum?"

"Yessum."

"You always said you'd do anything for me didn't you?"

"Yessum."

"Then go and look after my man till this war is over. God knows when that will be."

"I will, Miss Faith, and I's gonna bring him back to you when this heah war's over. No matter how long dat be."

Sensing the need for the two to be alone, Dagan with Lum in tow headed toward the boat. Gabe trying to hold his emotions in check, looked at Faith.

"I will always love you."

"And I you," Faith replied as Gabe embraced her. In doing so, he felt something hard against his chest. The ruby. They had overlooked it when he had been taken prisoner. He took it out and placed it in Faith's hand, "You have my heart in your hand, to hold till I return."

Taking the ruby, Faith grasped it tight in her fist, and then said, "I'll not let it go."

Gabe kissed her then turned and made his way to the boat, choking back his emotions once more. Nanny had been standing back, watching. She walked up and put a shawl over Faith's shoulders.

"Yo mama would skin you alive child, being out heah in this night air half-naked as you is."

Faith still held the ruby in her hand and could feel the heat it exuded. Then quietly she said, "There goes the man I love, Nanny."

"Mine too, child, mine too."

PART THREE

The Prize

Yonder ships a privateer
With men and guns a plenty
What say you my brave men
Shall we take this enemy
Reduce all sail, run out the guns
Put one across her bow
Yonder ship will be our prize
Before the quarter hour

...Michael Aye

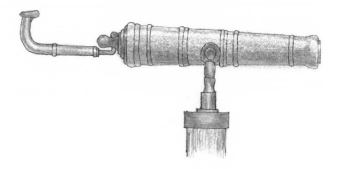

Chapter One

Lum proved his value immediately in guiding the boat into the channel through the marsh and into and down Broad River. As quietly and quickly as possible they went past Port Royal then out into the bay. The tide had been on the ebb as Caleb had warned. The boat Jubal and Kawliga commandeered was the *Lucky Lady*, a yawl, a fishing boat of twenty-five feet in length and six feet in width. It had two masts, a mainmast and a small mizzenmast that was located right on the transom. It also was equipped for four sets of oars. The boat was overcrowded. Thirteen people with a few supplies.

However, Gabe wished for one more. Without thinking, he clutched the leather bag around his neck— the empty bag. He went to remove it from around his neck but stopped. He would keep it there. The bag would remain close to his heart. Like his heart…empty until…until.

"Better come a point or two larboard," Dagan called. He was in the bow and Gabe sat at the tiller.

Casting aside his personal sorrow, Gabe called forward, "Let's set the sails and see how she does. We may have to rearrange either the supplies or where people are sitting."

The girls were huddled together. Little thought had been given to how they were dressed when they were freed and herded down the boardwalk and into the boat. The girls were shivering from the cool damp night air. The men had given what they could in the way of clothing but some of the girls had been almost naked, so even with the clothing a lot of skin was still exposed to the elements and the men's eyes.

Especially Jubal, who was feasting his eyes. Gabe had caught him staring more than once, but what did you say to a young boy. Gabe smiled to himself, thinking of the bent up humours the boy must be suffering from.

The girls who had been silent when they first escaped had started to talk. It was amazing to Gabe as he listened to the chatter that most of them were from the Tidewater area in Virginia but did not know each other. One was a strawberry blonde from Boston and appeared to be whiter, almost pale in skin colour. The girls all seemed to come from fairly well to do colonial families but had nothing else in common, except each had been sexually abused by Adam Montique. He seemed to enjoy acting out different scenarios while Hindley would cheer him on and on occasion take part himself.

The strawberry blonde girl was named Erin. She had been singled out by Hindley and had suffered more abuse than the others. Dagan seemed to sense her need and talked quietly with the girl who sobbed at times. Gabe knew if anyone could help her it was Dagan.

The one thing Gabe found strange was that with all the women on board Caleb seemed distant. Generally, Caleb would have been showing an interest and making himself as irresistible as possible. Was he showing the girls respect because of their recent ordeal? Was he having pain from the recent snake bite? Something was different.

Little did Gabe know Caleb's mind was on a woman, but not one of these. But one that was tucked away in Virginia. One named Kitty.

"Sail ho!" Dagan called out. Half dozing at the tiller, Gabe was instantly alert.

"Where?"

"Two points off the starboard bow."

Without rocking the boat, Gabe stood up. He couldn't see a thing. The sun was coming up and that made it even more difficult.

"You sure?"

For an answer Dagan just gave him a look. *Dumb question*, Gabe thought. It had been three nights and two days since they'd made their escape. This was the dawn of the third day. They had discussed putting in at Charlestown but it was agreed it would be safer for Gabe and Dagan to sail on toward Norfolk.

Hopefully, they would meet up with Markham and the *Swan*. He was to have cruised these waters hoping for a rendezvous, but that would be a chance meeting only. The likelihood that the sail was British was good, but it could just as well be a colonial ship.

However, after three days and nights in a small boat the wear on the girls was starting to show. The fair-skinned Erin in particular was showing the effect of constant exposure to the sun and wind. If a meeting with a ship had not occurred by midday Gabe had already decided to put ashore. The winds had been light and at times almost nonexistent, but Gabe knew they had to have made enough progress to be off the coast of North Carolina.

After another fifteen minutes Dagan called back, "She's British and looks like a mail packet or dispatch ship."

Not wanting to be missed, Gabe had Rud fire off three shots. *That should wake up the buggers*, he thought. However, there had been no cause for concern.

The lookout on the mail packet, *Parrott*, had already called down his sighting, "Sail ho! Dead ahead, boat load of naked women."

***

Lieutenant Farnsworth Dean of *HMS Parrott* was most accommodating, as was his only other officer and the entire ship's crew. It was not everyday you picked up a boat load of naked, well, near naked women. The lifetime dream of all sailors.

Dean listened intently as Gabe related his story. When the *Swan* was mentioned, Dean related they had sighted *Swan* and talked with her commander two days ago. So they had in fact been keeping a sharp lookout. Dean surprised Gabe by telling him he had been a midshipman under then Captain Gilbert Anthony on *HMS Recourse*, and recounted their battle with Algerian pirates, "It was a hot time we had of it that day."

"Mr Buck made me promise to take care, so he wouldn't have to send me home in halves. Ha! Ha! I hear he's a post captain now and Captain Anthony has raised his flag," Dean continued.

"Aye," Gabe said, realizing how much he missed his brother and his own ship, the *SeaWolf*. How he longed to be back in his cabin. He needed the ship to take his mind off Faith. It appeared Dagan's lady luck had finally changed. Not only changed but also played a cruel trick as far as Gabe was concerned. He couldn't come to grips with the many thoughts that were running through his head. He could resign his commission and maybe that would change her mind. But no, he couldn't do that. He couldn't dishonour Gil or his father, no matter what.

Dean, seeing Gabe was lost in thought excused himself to give Gabe some much needed time alone. Gabe didn't even realize Dean had gone on deck. It was the sound of music that brought Gabe out of his deep thought. A soft sound, a pleasant but a mournful sound.

As Gabe stood up to investigate the noise, he banged his head on an overhead beam. "Damn," he cried aloud without thinking. The lick caused tears to come to his eyes.

Dagan came in just as the incident happened, "Clear your thoughts did you?"

"More like muddled them for good I'm thinking," Gabe replied still rubbing his head. "What's that sound?"

"It's Lum playing a lotz."

"Damned if he didn't pick a sad tune."

"To fit your mood?"

"Well, it doesn't miss it far. Dagan...I don't know what to do. There she was, as good as mine, happy, then her mood changed and like quicksilver she was gone. Can you guess why, Dagan? I've never asked for anything for me, but tell me...will she be there Dagan? Will she be there when this is over?"

Dagan sensed the pain in his nephew, knew he needed something to hold on to but he couldn't bring himself to make a promise that this war could change.

"I'll think on it Gabe, I don't have a true feeling right now, but I do know if the love is true, true like the Admiral's and Maria's, then only death can come between you."

After standing still a long silent moment, Gabe asked, "What's a lotz?"

Unable to hide his smile Dagan explained, "A lotz is a type of flute. Lum made it himself out of boxwood. He said the first one he made was out of river reeds but this one's a touch more elaborate."

"It's a pretty sound, Dagan, but that was definitely a sad tune."

Dagan then looked directly at Gabe, "Could be Lum is missing someone too."

***

"Sail ho, bearing down amidships to the starboard, looks like the *Swan*, sir."

Dean had a tight ship and a sharp, experienced lookout; he called down his sighting without having to be prompted for more information.

Hearing the sighting excited Gabe. Markham. He had missed his friend. The two had been very close ever since they had been midshipmen together.

It took another turn of the glass before *Swan* was alongside *Parrott*. Dean had bent on the signal "missing flock returned" so Markham had himself rowed over to *Parrott*. After much good-natured ribbing and back slapping Markham was introduced to the rest of the missing flock.

"Lieutenant Francis Markham, ladies, Captain of *HMS Swan*." As the girls were introduced, now more appropriately attired, Gabe caught Markham staring at Erin.

Well, he ain't dead, he thought, still not understanding the change in Caleb and his mannerisms where the women were concerned. Everyone made a big deal out of Kawliga and Jubal. Rud grunted a lot but wasn't that talkative. Lum was silent and seemed nervous about the attention he was being paid. Gabe made up his mind to talk with Lum first chance he had when the two could be alone.

It was decided Markham would take all of Gabe's party aboard *Swan* and head toward Nova Scotia and Lord Anthony. *Parrott* would return southward to Saint Augustine and then to the West Indies.

It was a happy and cheerful Mr Davy that greeted Gabe, Dagan, Caleb, and the rest of the group as they came aboard *Swan*. Once everything had been stowed, Davy got the ship underway.

"Not a sniffling little snit anymore, is he?" Markham asked his friend.

"Nay," Gabe answered, "He's always been a brave one. He'll go far if he's not killed."

"Rud, where can we put you ashore?" Gabe and Markham had been discussing their human cargo. It didn't make sense to take them all the way to Nova Scotia. Therefore Rud was called in for advice.

"Where are we now?" the soldier asked.

"Close to North Carolina," Markham replied.

"I'd be obliged if you could drop me off at Wilmington," Rud said. "I got kin there and after a visit I'll mosey on back down to Colonel Marion. You two share the same name," Rud said speaking to Markham. "Him being Francis Marion and you being Francis

Markham. Course you don't look alike, him being from South Carolina and you being a Britisher and such."

Gabe could barely control his smile as a somewhat taken aback Francis Markham agreed to put a boat ashore off Wilmington circumstances permitting.

After Rud stood to leave he addressed Gabe, "If all Britishers were like you and Dagan I doubt we'd be warring. I'm obliged to have met you and was glad to have helped sprung you from your fix. Don't worry about your little lady; we'll keep our ears and eyes out for her. We'll also put out the word on Montique. Maybe Colonel Marion will pay him a personal visit."

***

A stiff breeze was blowing when Gabe made his way on deck at dawn. Seeing him, Mr Harrell, *Swan's* first lieutenant, nudged his captain.

Markham, looking at Gabe, said, "I thought you might sleep in this morning."

"No," Gabe replied. "Old habits die hard."

Instantly Markham knew Gabe longed for his ship. Was it always so? A woman, a ship, but always a longing.

"The master says the winds will die some at first light. He expects a sunny day but relates it will get colder as we continue northward."

"Not like those warm days at Antigua is it, my friend?" Gabe asked.

"Nay, but that's in the past, Gabe, it's best to think on today."

At six bells the bosun piped up hammocks. After the men rolled their hammocks, they were sent to wash and scrub the weather decks with holystones, then flog them dry. Most of the men had a substantial appetite by the time the cook and his mates had the galley fires lit and breakfast was piped.

Markham had never been a fast eater and felt the men should have time to enjoy their meals so he allowed one glass for breakfast. Thirty minutes was more than enough time for most men to eat their oatmeal gruel and still have time for a chew or bowl of tobacco.

***

"Sail ho! Two sails off the larboard beam."

"Damn early for company is it not, Mr Davy?"

"Aye, Mr Harrell, that it is. Should I inform the captain, sir?"

"I'm sure he heard the hail, but we'll follow protocol. My compliments to the captain and there's two strange sails off the larboard beam."

"No need, Mr Harrell, I'm here."

"Aye, sir."

"Anything further?"

"Not yet, sir."

"Mr Davy, be so kind as to take a glass aloft. It appears our man aloft doesn't have as good a set of peepers as Quinn did yesterday," Markham ordered.

"Aye, sir. I'll report right away," Davy replied, and then clambered up the shrouds, shunning the lubber's hole as he gained the lookout's platform.

"Deck there," Davy shouted. "Two schooners, sir."

"He didn't waste any time, did he?" Lieutenant Harrell commented.

"Experience, Mr Harrell, experience. I trained, er...Lieutenant Anthony and I trained that boy ourselves," Markham corrected himself as he noticed Gabe's gaze upon him.

"Deck there," Davy called down again, "Appears to be two colonials, sir."

"Well, that puts paid in putting a boat ashore," Markham replied.

Something Rud had said, however, gave Gabe something to consider. But this was Markham's ship, not his, so they'd have to discuss it.

"Captain Markham?"

The official use of his title caused Markham to turn toward his friend, "Yes?"

"May I have a word with you, please?"

"Now?

"Aye, sir."

"Very well. Mr Harrell, keep a close look out." Markham ordered as he strode aft to confer with Gabe.

"Damme sir, but have you been in the sun too long? Has your brain been completely fried?" Markham asked after hearing Gabe's plan.

"Listen, Francis, it's a way to get our passengers ashore and put out the word on Montique at the same time."

"Playing the devil's advocate," Markham asked, "What makes you so sure they'll act as you suppose?"

"Come on, Francis, wouldn't you at least initially honour a flag of truce?"

"Gabe, how is it I know you're scheming when you use my first name?"

"I don't know."

"Because you do it every time. Sure as hell when there's a chance to end up arsehole over elbows you always use Francis. Come on Francis, there's nothing to it Francis. Well, let me tell you something, Mr Gabriel Anthony, if there's a court martial and we wind up on the beach you have just acquired another mouth to feed."

Surprised, Gabe exclaimed, "You'll do it? That's my Francis." To which Markham rolled his eyes and shook his head and groaned, "Ohh....h"

Back on deck, Markham called Mr Harrell, "Bend on a flag of truce. Mr Davy, get ready to launch a long boat. Lieutenant Anthony is going on a rowing expedition."

Both Harrell and Davy looked shocked, but both turned to do their bidding without question. Markham then turned to the bosun, "Reduce sail."

Mr Harrell then reported, "Flag on truce bent on as ordered, sir."

"Very well, Mr Harrell, now have one of the starboard cannons fired. Unshotted, Mr Harrell"

By the time the cannon had been fired hoping to attract attention to the flag of truce, Gabe and Rud were getting into the longboat with Erin in company. As the three made their way from the ship, Markham felt a sense of regret. Erin as well as the rest of the ladies had dined with him and Gabe, but for some reason he hated to see that one go.

Before reaching the larger of the two schooners, Gabe noted that a boat had put out from the smaller ship and apparently her captain had been rowed across.

Both schooners were sleek, nimble, well-handled vessels. Their captains knew their business no doubt and Gabe couldn't help but think they'd present a tough pair in a battle. There was no doubt the two would wreak havoc on British shipping and make a nice profit for themselves as privateers.

"Permission to come aboard," Gabe called out as his boat bumped into the hull of the larger ship. As Gabe climbed the ladder he heard a thud and a splash. Rud had misjudged his step and now his left leg dangled in the cold Atlantic.

"Better have the lady wait on a bosun's chair," was called down from above. Gabe made his way through the entry port onto the deck, and then turned to lend Rud a hand before introducing himself. He had borrowed clothes from Markham, so at least he was presentable this time, he thought, recalling the slave clothing he'd been wearing when he tried to introduce himself to Montique.

"Lieutenant Gabriel Anthony," Gabe said, introducing himself before allowing the ship's captain to question him. "This is Mr Rud. He's part of Colonel Francis Marion's South Carolina brigade, and the lady is Miss Erin Lancaster from Boston."

The two captains then introduced themselves. "I'm Captain Jack Cunningham and welcome aboard the *Norfolk Gold*. This is Captain Malachi Mundy and that's his *Willing Maid* you see there. We are out of the tidewater area."

Gabe noticed he hadn't been specific as to exactly where.

"Now what do we have of such importance that a Navy Lieutenant is willing to surrender, shots unfired."

"Truce sir, not surrender, just a momentary truce that I feel will be most beneficial for both of us, should you allow me but a quarter hour of your time."

It was a full hour before Gabe, Captains Cunningham and Mundy, Rud, and Erin returned on deck. Gabe had told his story in full then stepped aside as Rud and then Erin had both been questioned. She had brought out something that Gabe had forgotten to mention. Not only were Cunningham and Mundy from Tidewater but so were the rest of the women. Erin had been the only one from a different area. These bits of information seem to make the two privateer captains more determined to lend a hand.

"We'll send this one home," Cunningham said as he put his hand across Rud's shoulder, "And we'll make sure the women are cared for and protected until they can be reunited with their families."

"We'll also put out the word on Montique," Mundy volunteered. "A treacherous soul that one and one to watch if I'm any kind of judge. You be careful, Lieutenant Anthony. That man will soon be ruined, both his reputation and finances. A man like that will hold a grudge and try to hurt you any way possible even if it's with your missy that went to Savannah." This thought gave Gabe a chill.

As Gabe made his way over the side, Captain Mundy spoke again, "I hope the *Willing Maid* and your *SeaWolf* never come to blows. You're a honourable man and I like you."

"Aye," Cunningham chimed in, "We'd not like to battle you, but we will if we must."

As the girls were being loaded into the longboats, Gabe talked with Lum. "Rud says you can go with him and Colonel Marion will make you free after the war. Captain Cunningham also says he has a place for you and you'd be a free man. Your other option is to stay with me. You can either be signed on as a crew member or you can be my servant, and you'll be paid as a free man."

Lum looked very solemn. "You don't wants to be rid of me do ya, suh?"

"No, Lum, you know better." [3]

"Well, I wouldn't want to be fighting against you if I can help it. I can make do on the rivers, sloughs, and backwaters around Port Royal but I ain't much count when it comes ta being a deep water sailor, so's I guess I'll just be yo servant. You is going after Missy Faith after the war, ain't ya?"

"I sure am, Lum, I sure am."

"Well, we's best stay together then, suh. I'll be yo servant till we see Missy Faith and Nanny again. Now what can I do foh ya as yo servant dat is?"

"Teach me to play the lotz, Lum. I want to learn to play it."

After his talk with Lum, Gabe went to say his goodbyes to the girls and Rud. Dagan was talking to Kawliga and Jubal so Gabe made his way over to their group to thank them. Just as he was approaching he heard Caleb say to Jubal, "I have a letter here for Kitty. See that she gets it, will you?"

"I will," Jubal promised, then as a youth will do asked the all important question, "Are you sweet on her, Caleb?"

"Aye, lad, that I am," Caleb answered very sincerely without hesitating.

Well, I'll be damned, Gabe thought as Caleb's actions suddenly made sense.

Chapter Two

The following day was no different from most days at sea. Overnight the wind had backed some, but it was still "a soldier wind." The schooner's sails were impressive and Markham knew how to handle the *Swan*.

They were on a heading almost due north. The water along the leeside seemed to be rushing past as evidence of the ship's progress. *Seven knots at least*, Gabe thought. It was almost as if the ship couldn't wait to join the rest of Lord Anthony's squadron.

It was rejuvenating to feel the wind and the motion of the ship as it climbed a wave only to dip its bow into a trough then rear up to meet another wave. The occasional spray that came amidships was refreshing even if it did cause the sunburn on Gabe's face to sting somewhat. After all the frustrations and pain suffered these past few weeks, Gabe couldn't help but question himself. Did he do right by leaving the convoy to go after a single ship? Admiral Gayton had stressed the need for the gunpowder. "Britain is hamstrung by these damnable shortages" had been Gayton's words. But would they hold up in a court martial? At least he could say he kept it from the colonials. *But what about Gil? What would his reaction be*, Gabe wondered? Would he have acted as he had done? Or would Gil have stayed with the convoy? Gabe knew Gil had stretched matters by putting Markham aboard the *Swan* and sending her on dispatch without ever sending her through the prize courts.

He would be given some discretion as an admiral, but if the truth of the real mission to rescue Gabe was ever publicized, then like his father Gil may have to haul down his flag and retire. The thought sent an involuntary shudder through Gabe.

"You cold?"

Gabe had not been aware of Caleb and Dagan as they walked up on him. He now sat in their shadow.

"You cold?" Caleb repeated.

"Could be the smell of the galley," Dagan spoke without giving Gabe a chance to respond to Caleb. Continuing, Dagan said, "Smells like greasy slush. Just what we need to put some meat back on those bones, boiled beef hacked into a mixture of soggy ship's biscuits with a little slush on top. That'll put the weight back on you."

"Or kill him one," Caleb chimed in as he set on the bulwark.

Dagan squatted between them, and took out his pipe, and filled his bowl, speaking softly, "It's a hard time we have ahead of us but I've a feeling you two will find what you're looking for."

Neither Caleb nor Gabe spoke as Dagan put his back to the wind, and with cupped hands soon had his pipe lit, sending an aromatic smell down the length of the ship which all but overcame the odour from the galley funnel.

Another shadow appeared, causing the group to look up. It was Lum. He squatted next to Dagan and lit his own pipe. Not a meerschaum like Dagan's but a simple corncob pipe with a straight stem. As the four sat together, *Swan* made her way up the coast in a ghostly silent manner.

Looking to larboard, Lum said what they were all feeling. "They's watching us, they knows we heah! Trouble is we don't know what they's about." Then Lum took his lotz from inside his shirt and after licking his lips played another of his sad melodies.

Looking at the black man whose black hair gleamed from ocean spray and specks of gray, Gabe thought, *Damned if he doesn't have the uncanny knack of playing a tune to fit my mood.*

Later that night as the sky darkened, the men off watch slung their hammocks and everybody seemed to be in his own world. Gabe lay down in his cot in the captain's cabin. Markham had been very gracious, sharing his cabin with him. Lying there, the familiarity of the ship seemed to ease his troubled mind. While he wasn't back on the *SeaWolf,* he was at sea in an environment in which he knew and was comfortable in. This was the salve his soul needed.

***

The dawn broke with the promise of a much different day. Davy, bright and cheerful as ever, sidled up to Gabe, "Master says we'll get wet today."

"Well, I'd never question the master," Gabe replied, rubbing the sleep from his eyes. Years of service at sea made him an early riser…but he'd never be a good riser.

Seeing Gabe on deck, Markham walked over to his friend. "Get the cobwebs cleared yet?" Gabe's answer was a yawn.

"Nantucket is off to larboard," Markham explained, "I want to stay well out so we won't have to play errand boy to some self important captain or another admiral. If all goes well, we should meet up with Lord Anthony tomorrow."

Towards noon the master's prediction came true. A heavy drizzle started and the sky turned gray matching the sea that was getting up. Markham crossed the deck and the man at the wheel volunteered, "She be steady, sir, nor' by east, full and bye."

Markham nodded and seemed to be on edge. "Massachusetts is home to some of the most able privateers. We can't let our guard down this close to home. While you were...ere...in the southern colonies Gabe, a dispatch schooner was headed to New York and was taken by the brigantine, *Trannicide*, fourteen guns. Her Captain Fisk is without a doubt a capable man."

"Deck there! Sail, no, two sails dead ahead off the starboard bow."

Gabe and Markham both gave a knowing look to each other. "Mr Davy!"

"On my way, Captain." Davy didn't wait to be told. Upon hearing the sighting he'd grabbed a glass and was making his way towards the shrouds before Markham could call out.

Looking at Gabe, Markham said, "Cheeky little bugger. Thinks he has me figgered out, does he?"

"Aye, that he does," Gabe replied noticing Dagan headed toward him with Lum in tow.

"It's a brigantine grappled to another ship, sir, maybe a corvette."

Dagan and Gabe looked at one another, could it be the same ship they'd met off the South Carolina border?

"Are you sure, Mr Davy?"

"Aye, sir, I'm sure and it's a fight they're having, I'm thinking. You can see muzzle flashes."

"Very well," Markham replied, then turning to Lieutenant Harrell, "Beat to quarters if you will, sir. It appears we've work to do today."

Harrell stood by the wheel while Gabe and Markham discussed the strange sail. Would the corvette, if that was what she truly was, recognize *Swan*? Would her captain know she had been taken? These were all questions that passed between Gabe and Markham; questions but no answers. However, in these waters you could choose a dozen possibilities and all spelled trouble.

"Deck there! She's definitely a corvette, sir." Well, if Davy was that sure, then they had a fight on their hands.

"She'll have twenty guns at least," Markham replied.

"Aye," Gabe answered, "But if we've seen them then likely the schooner she attacked has spotted us as well so maybe that will put the odds in our favour."

"We'll know soon enough, I imagine," Markham answered and then turned his voice to the lookout, "Keep watching her, Davy."

Gabe waited for the deck to steady as *Swan's* bow dipped through a swell and then he trained his glass on the two ships. They were close enough now. Individuals could be made out. With only a small crew, *Swan* would be hard put to give a good accounting for herself.

With Gabe, Dagan, Lum, and Caleb the total number on board was only seventy-six. She needed ninety to properly fight. Gabe was sure the privateer had double their number on board. He hoped the schooner would have enough survivors left to lessen the odds.

"You going to close and fight her, sir?" said Lieutenant Harrell.

Markham's reply was short and terse, "Would you have me turn our heels and abandon yonder ship, sir?"

Experience, Gabe thought. *The man lacked experience.*

It had never occurred to Markham to do anything but fight. It was his duty.

The gunner approached Markham, knuckled his forehead and announced, "Cleared for action sir, all guns loaded."

Swan carried fourteen six-pounders and half a dozen swivels. The *Swan* was now on a converging tack, bowsprit to bowsprit, like two knights engaging in a joust. Dagan was on deck now bringing with him Gabe's sword and pistols. So near the admiral's squadron, yet so far away. Lum was with Dagan, seeing him Gabe felt a pang of sorrow for this man involved in a war where regardless of who won his station in life would differ but little.

"Lum."

"Yes, suh."

"You do not have to fight this battle. You can go below until it's over."

"You's going to fight ain't ya, Mister Gabe?"

"Aye, Lum, that I am, but it's my duty."

"Well, suh, it's my duty to watch over you like I done promised Missy Faith I'd do. So we's both got our duties to do."

Gabe knew it would be pointless to try to dissuade the man farther. He instead turned to Dagan, "Help Lum pick out a good weapon."

"Aye," Dagan replied. Then as the two walked off Gabe had another thought.

"Lum."

"Yes, suh?"

"We aren't fighting masters, plantation overseers, or white men, we're fighting the enemy, do you understand that? A man's colour doesn't matter."

"Yes, suh, I understand, it's kill or be kilt."

After Lum and Dagan went to collect weapons for themselves, Gabe approached Markham. "Francis, what would you have me do? I'm at your disposal."

Despairingly Markham shook his head, "It's a fool's errand, Gabe. How can we do anything but make a gesture. However, we've been in worse shapes haven't we, old friend?"

"That we have," Gabe replied.

"I'm about to fire the forward guns then have the rest of the guns fire as we come abreast. The swivels are loaded with grape. I figure our only chance is to grapple and board. We'll never stand a chance against twenty twelve-pounders. I was going to send Harrell forward and I was going to position my party amidships. If you're bound to get yourself shot at you can take a party aft. With hope on our side, we'll meet in the middle."

"We'll meet," Gabe responded and shook Markham's hand, "Take care, my friend, have a care."

***

"Take in the mainsail, Mr Harrell. Run up the colours, Mr Davy. Fire as you bear. Let's give them a taste of British steel."

Markham was right. The privateer was heavily armed and there was a score of men on deck. The forward gun went off and someone fired a swivel at the same time, a double percussion…BOOM! BANG!…startled Gabe.

Then one by one, *Swan's* remaining six guns fired. However, the enemies' guns were not silent, and with a thunderous crash a hole was blasted through forward, uplifting the number one gun that landed on its side crushing several crewmen. A gaping hole was now where a gun port had been. Shot after shot ploughed into the *Swan*. Most however went high, as consideration had not been taken of the fact that *Swan* being a smaller ship set lower in the water. The starboard bulwark had taken a beating with only a few sections left standing. The mainmast had a gash in it that sent splinters flying and blinding one of the bosun mates. Riggings were taken a beating but so far everything that was supposed to be aloft was still aloft.

He could now hear the shouts and curses as men fought. The schooner's people gave a cheer as *Swan's* hull dug into the privateer's hull and come to a grinding halt. Grapnels were heaved and while some were being made tight, others were used by men to swing over and climb up the bigger ship.

Gabe, Dagan, Lum, and a group all boarded onto the bow of the corvette. A group of cursing men was waiting, and with screams and threats the two groups collided. Lum met his attacker first and a wicked blow from a boarding axe caused a handspike to clatter on deck as the man holding it found his hand was now only holding on to his arm by a small piece of flesh. Screaming, he broke and ran.

Gabe found himself fending off a rogue who knew how to handle a cutlass; however he was too aggressive and fell for a feint Gabe made which opened his guard and Gabe's sword plunged into the man's armpit causing blood to spurt. Startled shouts and musket shots seemed to be coming from every direction.

Gabe suddenly became angry, wildly angry. All the vented frustrations seem to let loose at once. A man with a bayoneted musket tried to fire only to realize he'd not reloaded after firing the last shot, so he lunged at Gabe with the bayonet that Gabe deftly deflected, and then he shot the man with his pistol. He then ducked as a man slashed at him with a blade only to fall to Lum's axe.

"This way men, this way, *Swannies*," that was Markham rallying the men. Another loud sound from amidships, a swivel had been fired. Looking across the privateer's deck, Gabe realized that what looked like a pile of rubbish was actually dead bodies.

Another privateer brandishing a boarding pike and pistol attacked Dagan. Slipping in blood Dagan fell causing his own weapon to go off taking the top of the man's skull off. Above the den of clashing steel, musket and pistol shots, screams, and curses Gabe could hear the sudden cheers of men. Theirs or ours, he wondered.

"To midships," he called to his group, "Make your way to midships." As the fight continued, the battle seemed less furious. Davy stood over a man rolling on the deck; his dirk was sticking from the man's chest. Blood ran down Davy's hand. As the man tried to raise and fire his pistol Dagan raised a boarding pike and crashed it down across the man's skull.

"Dat one was already dahyd and jus didn't know it," Lum declared.

Struggling over upended guns Gabe realized *Swan's* guns did more than he had first thought. The fighting had all but ended, as Gabe's group made their way past sprawled bodies and wounded men crawling, begging for help.

Then suddenly one last group of privateers seemed to rise up in defiance. Their leader swung a boarding axe that made a swooshing sound as Gabe ducked under its blade. As he ducked he lost his footing and landed heavy on his backside only to be jerked up by Dagan who quipped, "No time for sitting down on the job now."

The man who swung the blade was now on the deck in a big puddle of blood. When Gabe looked further the man appeared to have a third eye. One created by a musket ball courtesy of *Swan's* marine sharpshooters. Now that the resistance had almost ended, Gabe's group made their way to Markham's group. Markham turned to greet Gabe when Davy shouted, "Look out sir!" Just in time Markham jumped backwards. His attacker had sliced open his coat with a heavy cutlass. Markham felt an instant burning sensation to his stomach and felt a warm wetness when he touched the area with his hand. Then the man with his blade held high above his head yelled a curse and lunged at Markham.

Using his own blade to take the brunt of the blow a numbing shock seemed to penetrate his shoulder. As the two blades clashed a sudden fear gripped Markham, and with a bloody hand he removed his knife from his belt. His attacker, a much bigger man, was filled with blood lust and seemed to be ignorant that the battle was lost. Once again, raising his cutlass in an arc over his head the man swung his blade with all his might. Had the aim been true it would have killed, but again Markham used his blade to deflect the other's cutlass, but this time he only partially deflected the blade and by giving some and side-stepping, his opponent became off balance and fell forward exposing his flank. As he did so Markham drove his knife blade deep to the hilt, right into the man's kidney. The man fell into a pile then as one, the *Swannies* broke into cheers. The tired but jubilant men clapped their friends' backs and shook each other's hands.

"So we can't do anything but make a gesture," Gabe asked recalling Markham's words. "Well, damme, sir, but I think we just made one hell of a gesture."

"Aye," Markham replied, "But we couldn't have done it without your help."

"Cap'n!"

"Yes, Mr Davy."

"The brigantine's captain requests to see you, sir, but he's wounded so you'll have to go to him."

"Very well. Where's Mr Harrell?"

"He's…ah…he's been wounded, sir," Davy replied with a snicker.

"Something about Mr Harrell being wounded humours you, sir?"

"Aye, Cap'n, when he was boarding he slipped and fell on the prong of a grappling hook."

"Is his injury serious, Mr Davy?"

"I...don't...think so, but it's the first time I ever seen a man grapple his own arse, sir." The crew upon hearing Davy's words howled in laughter.

"Mr Davy!" Markham scowled at the youth while trying to suppress his own laughter. "You better hope the lieutenant is not laid up long because you'll be doing his duties."

As Gabe and Dagan turned away, Lum innocently asked, "What's he mean, grapple his arse?" Which set the crew to howling again. Turning, Gabe saw Markham giving him the eye, so he grinned, shrugged and went back to board the *Swan*.

***

Gabe was at the point of boarding the *Swan* when he heard a commotion. Turning he saw Davy with his pistol drawn at a man who was apparently trying to make his way below on the privateer. Since Markham was tending the schooner's captain, Gabe decided to investigate.

"What do we have here, Mr Davy?"

"Frenchman, sir, trying to slip below. He's slowly worked his way from midships to the companion ladder, sir. I thought his actions were suspicious, so I watched and stopped him as he was making his move to get below."

Dagan was patting the man down for weapons and found a key in the man's coat pocket. Turning to Gabe he said, "He's no crewman...officer...and more than likely he's the captain." The key on a gold chain swung from Dagan's hand emphasizing the suspicion.

Gabe nodded, "Go below and see if there's a magic box this key may fit."

"Aye," Dagan replied and taking Lum in tow headed down to the captain's cabin.

Gabe then turned his attention to the prisoner, "You are French?"

"Oui, m'sieu, I am from France."

"What ship is this?"

"She is *Le Frelon.*"

"The *Hornet,*" Gabe replied.

"Oui, the *Hornet.*"

"Well, m'sieu, I think she's stung her last British ship." The Frenchman seemed nonchalant and only shrugged.

"You commanded her?" Gabe asked.

"Oui, I've had the pleasure."

"Do you know you'll hang for this, your act of piracy?" Gabe continued.

"I think not," the man answered, "We are not pirates. We are privateers. I have a letter of marque from the Marine Committee in Philadelphia."

"What is your name," Gabe asked.

The Frenchman smiled, "Au, we have forgotten the courtesies, have we not? I am Capitaine Francois Robeaud." The man's continued use of the word *oui* and *au* was starting to anger Gabe who thought, "*oui hell!*" However, formalities required he be civil.

"I am Lieutenant Gabriel Anthony."

"Do you command the ship?" Robeaud asked, indicating the *Swan.*

"I do not, sir, that privilege belongs to Lieutenant Francis Markham. He is presently with the brigantine's captain."

It then occurred to Gabe that Markham should be present. "Mr Davy!"

"Aye, sir."

"Would you be so kind as to give my regards to Captain Markham and if convenient could he return to the prize."

"Aye, Cap'n…ere, sir."

"Bosun!"

"Sir?"

"As soon as the prisoners are well secured take a party and search this ship." Gabe ordered.

"Aye, sir," the bosun replied then gathering up a party made his way below.

Turning back to the corvette captain, Gabe said, "Tell your crew to behave and they will be treated fairly, otherwise …"

"I cannot, m'sieu."

"Well, you damn well better," Gabe growled, "Because I promise you, sir, that should they try any mischief or attempt to damage this vessel in any way they will be fired upon without any quarter. The choice is up to you."

"What choice is that?" Gabe turned to see Markham had arrived. He introduced Robeaud to Markham, and then explained his comments. Markham then faced Robeaud.

"As I recall, sir, your men threw down their arms but you never came forth and gave your formal surrender."

"Because I have not," Robeaud replied.

"It is with regret then, sir, that I deem your actions less than honourable and place you under arrest. Mr

Davy, see that the prisoner is properly secured on board the *Swan*."

"I protest," Robeaud cried. "This is absurd."

"Protest all you desire, Captain," Markham answered, "but arrested you are."

At that time, Dagan came back on deck. "I think we've found something of interest."

Turning, Gabe saw the obvious bulge in Dagan's pockets and Lum's shirt appeared to protrude. *Damn,* Gabe thought. *I hope Markham doesn't become interested in what's in their pockets and shirt.*

As Gabe and Markham went down to the captain's cabin Lum stood aside and then made his way back to the *Swan*. Letting Markham go ahead, Gabe whispered to Dagan, "Surely you're not turning Lum into a larsonist?"

"Just looking after retirement," Dagan answered, "*Our* retirement."

Dagan had indeed found a magic box in which the key fit. "Damme," Markham exclaimed after reading the first page of a bundle of papers that had been locked in the box. As he started reading the second page, he handed the first to Gabe who was just as astonished as Markham.

"Damme, sir, do you know what this means?"

"Aye," Markham replied. "I think we'd better get underway directly. After seeing these papers perhaps Lord Anthony will not ask if we found anything else of value."

"*Damn,*" Gabe thought eyeing Dagan and then replied, "We didn't, Francis, we didn't."

Long after putting the papers back in the box and locking it, the heading of the papers still burned in

Markham's brain. "Plans for the invasion and occupation of Nova Scotia."

***

It was midday when the lookout called down, "Sail off the larboard bow." *Swan, Le Frelon,* and the merchant brigantine all reduced sail until the sighting had been identified. It was the gun ketch, *Pigeon,* commanded by Lieutenant Kerry. *Pigeon* had just rounded Cape Sable on her way to rendezvous with Lord Anthony's squadron at Halifax.

"You gave me a start," Kerry said to Markham. "It's not often we see a French corvette in these waters. I was sure you were a group of privateers." After hearing of *Le Frelon's* capture Kerry was surprised to hear Gabe was acting as commander. "So he's not dead. Half the squadron believes he's alive, while the other half thinks he's dead. Lord Anthony made it plain when he put Lieutenant Earl in command of *SeaWolf*—it was only temporary—until Gabe returned. Some thought him daff but he was so positive I figured he knew something the rest of us didn't."

"Aye," Markham replied, "he knew Dagan, and if Dagan say's it, you can count on it."

***

It was a joyous greeting that Gabe and Markham found waiting on them as they glided into the harbour of Halifax. Not only were Gabe and Markham returning, but they were returning with a French corvette as a prize. The *Pigeon* had made all sail and alerted everyone to their soon arrival.

"The admiral is sure pacing," Lieutenant Herrod remarked to Captain Moffett.

"Aye, that he is," Moffett replied. "He said all along Gabe was alive, but I can't help but believe there was a nagging doubt. I'm glad for him. He sets some store in young Gabe. More like a son than a brother."

"There's Bart, Captain, I can just imagine his words, 'know'd 'e were alive; I's jus know'd it.'" Herrod had Bart down pat. His mimicking the admiral's cox'n made Moffett chuckle.

"I...ha! ha!...don't think I'd let Bart hear you, Mr Herrod...ha! ha!...not if you plan on staying around long enough to make captain."

As the *Swan* crept closer her battle wounds were obvious. A gaping void in her bulwark had not been replaced, nor were the scars in her mast that still had pieces of iron imbedded in it. The damaged rigging had been replaced and the new stood out in contrast to the older, more seasoned rigging. The decks had been washed down well after the battle, the water had poured thick and bloody as it ran down the scuppers. Now, it would be hard for a person to fully comprehend the fierceness of the battle.

But some knew and that was why the harbour was lined, not only with Lord Anthony's ships, but also with every type of boat imaginable—all shouting, cheering huzza...huzza. As Gabe stood on the corvette's quarterdeck, he caught a glimpse of his brother standing tall and rigid, then off came his hat in a bow...a salute. The reception the returning ships were getting caused Gabe to think of Antigua and how the islanders cheered when time after time Lord Anthony would return with one or more prizes. A sudden chilling wind caused a sail to pop and made Gabe think the cheering was the only thing similar to Antigua as he pulled his cloak closer. The damn weather certainly was not similar.

Chapter Three

Bart had the admiral's barge crewed and on their way before Gabe had dropped anchor. "Let's do it up proper like," an excited Bart had urged Lord Anthony. "Make 'um feel like they's dig-na-terries being picked up in the admiral's own barge. Then when the fuss is all over…me and Silas will cut out 'is gizzard for scaring the life outta us uns so."

Bart's sentiment mirrored his own Lord Anthony thought but it was hard to fill ill toward Gabe when he had been trying to do his duty. Turning toward the companionway, Lord Anthony spoke with the flag captain, "I'll be in my quarters, Dutch. You can escort our wayward young officer down after you're finished on deck. He seems to have picked up someone along the way so make him comfortable until I send for him."

"Aye, My Lord." Dutch had also noticed the tall black man Gabe seemed to be pointing out things of interest to.

Suddenly a very loud cheer went up accented with musket fire. Lord Anthony paused and turning back to Dutch questioned, "*SeaWolf?*"

"Aye, My Lord, their captain is back."

"I hope Earl won't take offense."

"Nay, My Lord. He and Gabe are close and from all appearances Gabe and Markham may have brought a ship for him."

Smiling, Anthony chided, "You'd promote Earl over your own first lieutenant, Dutch?"

"Nay, My Lord, not I, but you."

With a smile on his lips Lord Anthony made his way to his quarters. Not even the stamp of the marine sentry stirred his ire. "Silas, Silas damn your slow soul I want…"

"It's already done, sir. I's sent for your best wine, we's cutting up some cheese and setting out some bread and opening some preserves. It'll be just right for young Gabe, My Lord, and that's no error."

***

After greeting Gabe and Markham on deck, Captain Moffett had his cox'n take Lum in tow. Dagan and Bart made their own way, which was likely to end up in the admiral's pantry, Dutch thought. Then eyeing the bulging canvas dispatch pouch Markham was carrying he led the two down to the great cabin.

"Flag Cap'n, suh," The marine sentry barked out then stood aside to let the officers enter, careful not to be obvious, but eyeing Gabe to get a better feel for this man who caused such a stir. The gray streak in Gabe's hair caught the man's eye causing him to take a deep breath.

"Something wrong?" Gabe asked.

"No sir, just a vapour sir," the sentry lied and was glad the officers took no more notice.

Entering the cabin, Gabe had forgotten how large it was. Compared to *SeaWolf's* tiny cabin it was enormous. It was furnished as befitted an admiral. Lady Deborah had seen to that. Around the cabin in a semicircle were half a dozen leather covered armchairs of emerald green. A mahogany wine cooler was in the corner and a sideboard rack held at least a dozen cut glass decanters filled with different shades of liquid. Another rack held two swords; one had been Admiral Lord James Anthony's. Seeing his brother's gaze, Gil walked up to Gabe and putting an arm around his shoulder said, "It'll be yours one day." The two brothers hugged, then stepping back and clapping Gabe's shoulder Gil whispered, "We'll talk later."

Then, switching from the role of concerned brother to that of concerned admiral, Lord Anthony spoke out, "Well, Captain, it's time we got down to business, is it not?"

"Aye, My Lord," Dutch answered, not fooled by his admiral's stiffness. "It appears we can't let the two of them out of our sight without them stealing a ship off some poor soul."

Glancing up as the group took seats in the leather armchairs, Lord Anthony saw Dagan and Bart enter the pantry where Silas waited. *No doubt Dagan's report to Bart as they enjoyed a wet would be more enlightening than what he'd get in written reports. Oh well, Bart would fill him in later.*

***

Lord Anthony listened closely as Gabe explained in detail about the convoy that had been placed in his charge. He told how resistant the *Turtle's* captain had been to obeying procedures and orders. Gabe explained why he believed that *Turtle's* commander had been a traitor and had in fact proven himself to be a traitor when Gabe had caught him red-handed unloading gunpowder for the rebels. "Gunpowder the British

Navy and its army needed badly." Lord Anthony didn't fail to notice the changes in Gabe's voice and demeanour as he told of the beautiful girl, who along with her nanny and Lum had rescued him and nursed him back to health, only to be imprisoned by another traitorous son of a bitch. Adam Montique, a traitor to both sides.

"You will recall, sir," Gabe spoke to Admiral Anthony, "Mr Montique was a very wealthy ship owner and planter in Antigua. It was he who loaned Commodore Gardner his home while he was the dockyard commissioner."

"As you suspected, sir," Gabe again addressed his brother specifically, "Someone was getting word to the pirates…it was Montique. He had several government contracts and with his frequent dealings with Commodore Gardner was able to keep the pirates well informed."

"You don't think Gardner was involved do you?" an unbelieving Captain Moffett asked.

"No sir," Gabe replied, "After being clubbed by one of Montique's men I was dragged to a warehouse and chained. Pretending to still be unconscious I listened while Montique bragged about how simple and stupid Gardner was…ah…No offense to the commodore, sir."

"None taken," Admiral Anthony replied. "Please continue."

"Aye, sir. Montique laughed at how trusting Gardner was. He talked Gardner into using his home stating it was better off being lived in; that way it was kept up. He stated his house was usually empty and at any rate when he was in Antigua he could stay in one of the guest rooms. That way he would still have accommodations when needed and Greta would have a comfortable place to live as long as Gardner was dockyard commissioner. If a contract came open what would it hurt for Montique to know about it? Gardner was persuaded and the rest is history."

"You mentioned earlier this Montique was a traitor to both sides," the Admiral spoke again, "How so?"

"Not only a traitor to both causes," Gabe replied, "But a white slaver as well." This caused Admiral Anthony and Captain Moffett to sit up.

"Damme sir, but did you say a white slave trader?" Moffett asked.

"Aye," Gabe replied, "He took young female captives from vessels the pirates plundered and then sold them to the Dey of Algiers. That is to say the ones Montique and his ruffians didn't use up for their own pleasure. God only knows what happened to those poor creatures after they were used."

Lord Anthony and Moffett looked dumbfounded as Gabe continued. "According to a man named Hindley, who was Montique's plantation overseer, if Faith...er... his niece, continued to avoid his advances, he was going to sell her to the Dey. Said a young blonde virgin would fetch a fortune...her weight in gold."

"His niece, incestuous bastard is he not?" Moffett exclaimed.

"Aye, sir. It was this Hindley who became so besotted with Faith's beauty he risked sure death by Montique when he attempted to rape the girl. It was then Lum killed the man and that made it necessary for me to bring him with me, for his protection. It was then Dagan showed up with his group and we escaped, taking the other captive girls with us. It's in the report, sir," Gabe said as he ended his story.

"Enlighten me if you will sir," Captain Moffett spoke again. "You've explained how Montique was an informer to the pirates and a slaver but how has he been a traitor to the colonials?"

"Well, sir," Gabe began again, "the Admiral can tell you that the pirates attacked all ships of means; it didn't matter if it was British, colonial, or what nation. It was a rich cargo he was after…whose made no difference. Even Commodore Gardner remarked on how a lot of those taken could have paid a large ransom. Well, Montique had the pirates kill the men, take pleasure in the…ah, older women, but the young girls and the younger the better, he sold into the Dey's harems. The goods from those ships he sold to the highest bidder, and then often had the ship waylaid carrying the cargo he'd just sold. Then he'd sell it again. His warehouse was full of contraband. There was enough in one warehouse to keep an entire Army going through a whole winter."

"I see," Moffett said.

After a brief pause, while Silas recharged everyone's wine glass, the report continued. This time both Gabe and Markham explained how the privateer had engaged the merchant vessel and how when they arrived the privateer was taken.

"Here's a list of cargo I thought would interest you, My Lord," Markham said as he proudly handed Lord Anthony an inventory list.

Taking a moment to go over the list the admiral raised his eyebrows. Then addressing the flag captain, he spoke. "Damme, Dutch, would you listen to this? After a one and a quarter hour engagement the privateer, *Le Frelon*...what's that...the wasp?"

"Hornet, sir," Markham corrected his senior, "*Le Frelon* means The Hornet."

"Yes well," the Admiral continued, "upon boarding her we found in cargo eight carriage guns, twelve swivel guns, twenty small arms, sixteen pistols, twenty cutlasses, some twenty cases of cartridges, boxes and belts for bayonets, nineteen barrels of powder, and nine half-barrels of powder. In addition, there were bales of blankets, crates of boots in assorted sizes, twelve kegs of rum, seven casks of naval wine, and a miscellany of shot and ball. We also captured a colonial captain, a sergeant and about twenty privates. Among the Army stores, we further found six three-pound cannons but no shot or ball. The captured vessel is a French built twenty-gun corvette in good repair. Her commander is a prisoner. We lost ten men killed, seven wounded, one of which is in a bad way."

"It is also my privilege," Markham spoke after the Admiral had finished reading the inventory, "to present this set of papers." Then handing an official document on parchment paper to Lord Anthony, Markham sat back and watched for the expression on the admiral's face to appear.

"My God, sirs," an excited and surprised Lord Anthony exclaimed. "Do you know what you have here...if...if mind you this document is real. Your discovery may have saved Nova Scotia."

Looking somewhat awed by His Lordship's words, Captain Moffett inquired as he reached out, "May I, sir?"

"Oh, forgive me, Dutch. Look at this."

As Moffett read the heading of the document his jaw dropped, *"The Plans for the Invasion and Occupation of Nova Scotia to be undertaken by a Consortium of Free Enterprise Ships and Vessels."* As Moffett read on he looked up, "Did you see the date, My Lord?"

"Aye, Dutch that I did."

"That doesn't give us much time to prepare a defence, sir."

"No, it doesn't. Are our patrol ships back in port, Dutch?"

"Aye, sir, all but *Merlin,* and she was due today."

"Make a signal for all captains to repair on board at 0800 on the morrow."

"Aye, sir, and sir have you decided about Mr Earl?"

"Yes, send for him immediately while I have my clerk draw up the orders." Then Lord Anthony stood. The formal interview was over. "We have a lot of preparation, gentlemen." Looking at Gabe and Markham he said, "Your find was a godsend. Have the privateer sent over to the flagship for further questioning."

"Do you think, sir," Markham asked, "that since we captured *Le Frelon*, they'll call it off?"

"I doubt it," Lord Anthony responded. "I doubt they know we've taken the ship yet and when they find out they will most likely figure the captain's papers were thrown overboard."

As the group made to leave, Lord Anthony put aside his admiral's demeanour as he spoke, "Gabe, would you do me the honour of dining with me tonight? Silas will have something to soothe the palate or I'll have him keel-hauled."

"Aye, sir, I would take pleasure in it."

"Good, now if you will give Earl time to gather his chest and report to me before you go aboard *SeaWolf*."

"Aye, sir, I'd not want to do anything to displeasure Mr Earl. We've been friends to long."

Smiling, Lord Anthony said, "And I imagine that friendship will continue for sometime since you're the one who helped capture the ship which will be his."

Gabe almost forgot himself, "Really Gil...er, sir, that's great. I'll spend some time with Bart and introduce him to Lum, if Dagan's not already done so."

"Very well," Lord Anthony explained, "I'd like to meet this Lum fellow soon myself."

As soon as Gabe had left, Lord Anthony called to Dagan..."You still in the pantry?"

"Aye, sir, I'm still here."

"Good, let me draft Earl's orders then we'll sit down and have a glass."

"Aye, My Lord, I do think I've something that will surprise you."

Looking at Dagan for a moment Lord Anthony replied, "I doubt it...I heard his voice when he mentioned her name."

***

Boarding *SeaWolf* again was exhilarating even if it did hold some foolish apprehensions. Apprehensions such as how had things gone since he'd been absent. Had Earl changed any of his standing orders or protocols? How was discipline and morale? Had the bosun sewed any red baize bags in his absence? Gabe couldn't recall *SeaWolf's* last flogging. Earl had spent time under Lord

Anthony long enough to know His Lordship believed in flogging only as a last resort.

"You ruin more good men than you know," he'd always say when he gathered his officers just prior to a commission. Why so many use it as intimidation was more than he could fathom.

Bart had used the admiral's barge again to row Gabe over to *SeaWolf*. That Hazard had been forewarned was obvious, probably by Earl, who had been summoned to the flagship. The entire crew had turned out in their best.

"Boat ahoy! *SeaWolf*!" The challenge and the reply, a bosun's pipe shrilled loudly filling the air as did cheers, then a firm "silence on deck." Gabe recognized the voice of Nathan Lavery.

As Gabe grabbed hold of the manropes and stepped out of the barge onto the batten a small swell leapt up between the two hulls and soaked his boat. *Damme, thought Gabe, what a way to board my own ship, leaving a wet footprint across the deck.*

As Gabe climbed through the entry port the cheers started again. *Huzza, Huzza...Huzza for the cap'n.* Hazard, the first lieutenant; Blake, the master; the second lieutenant, Lavery; the bosun, Carpenter; the gunner and even the purser were all turned out. Marine Lieutenant Baugean had the marines turned out as bright and shiny as if they were on parade. A grinning Sergeant Schniedermirer looked like he had two mouths. His grinning smile was upturned but age-old chew'bacy stains left a permanent downward appearance. Taking a step forward, Gabe took off his hat and gave a slight bow to the crew that set the men to howling all over again.

"Flattery, men, flattery, do you scallywags think such a welcome will get you any favours? Well, I'm sure none of you deserve it, but today…up spirits…for tomorrow there's work to be done."

The cheers broke out again and were almost deafening. Gabe had to almost shout to make himself heard, "Give me a few minutes, Mr Hazard, then I'd be pleased if you, the master, and Mr Lavery would report to my cabin."

"Aye, Captain."

"Damme," thought Gabe, *"That sounded good, to once again be addressed as captain."*

***

Gabe entered his cabin and felt a peace within him. Compared to his brother's great cabin it would be insignificant to many, but it was his private space. He recalled the first day he'd entered it. The deck above had been raised to give head room. A hatch with a sliding cover had been fixed to give extra daylight when the weather was permissive. His cabin was divided into three sections. To larboard, a section was set aside by a mahogany divider; his bed was a chest of four drawers not unlike a square box with a rim around the top to hold a feather mattress in place. His bed was suspended from the overhead by four one-inch ropes. This allowed the cot to swing as the ship rolled when in a heavy sea.

To the starboard side were his desk and chair. The starboard side was also divided off but the dividers were not nearly as elaborate as those on the flagship. Above the desk, sideboards had been built. Without realizing it,

Gabe ran his hands over the desk feeling the smooth well-oiled wood. The dark metal fasteners look aged and worn. There on the desk were the captain's standing orders. He'd spent hours preparing the orders only to throw half away after a conversation with his brother, who not only advised, but gave him two copies of his own orders—his first and a second much shorter version.

"The first was from my first command. The second was for *Drakkar*," Lord Anthony had explained. "Some captains make the mistake of putting too much in the orders and are forever being summoned. Others don't put enough and the consequence is the same because the men aren't sure what to do. Read these and adjust the orders to fit your ship and your needs. A half dozen absolute dos and don'ts are a good starting point."

No doubt father had given Gil the same advice, Gabe thought.

***

"A glass for you sir."

Gabe turned and Dawkins was standing by the divider. "Aye," Gabe replied, "And get yourself a glass. We have some things to talk over, you and I."

"I thought we might," the old seaman replied. He'd already seen the black man under Dagan's tow. Dawkins got his glass and sat in the armchair beside Gabe's desk. He listened as Gabe explained his commitment to Lum.

"What I thought we'd do," Gabe said, "is this. Lum was at one time a house servant. He's still in good health, but like someone else I know probably not fit for daily shipboard work."

"Aye, sir," Dawkins replied, "He's like me in that respect and I ain't 'shamed to say it. 'E's done seen the day he could splice and reef in all manner of seas."

"Right," Gabe answered, "Now what I envisioned is this. You will teach Lum your job, and then since you're an educated man, you will become my secretary."

"Aye, sir, I reckon it's time I used me learning so's it won't go to waste."

"Good," Gabe said. "It's settled." He had been concerned that Dawkins being a territorial old salt might not be as agreeable as Gabe had hoped he would be. However, captain's secretary was somewhat more of a status symbol than captain's servant so to Dawkins's way of thinking, he'd just got a promotion.

***

Thinking of the arrangement made Gabe think of Faith. Where was she? Did she go to Savannah as she said she would? Was she safe? Did she love him as he loved her? Did she really think of him as the enemy? He clutched the empty bag. Did she have the ruby? Was it next to her heart as she said it would be? The heart that had beat against his heart. The feel of her breast on his chest as they embraced. The feel of her breath against his face. The smell of her fresh-washed body. Her hair in his hand as his arms went around her. That kiss, those burning lips that caused flames of desire to rage through his body. "*My God*," Gabe thought, "*she has seized my very soul.*"

Little did Gabe know some seventeen hundred miles south, a blonde-haired girl sat in the porch swing of a three-story mansion looking out at the giant oak trees filled with low hanging moss. A gentle breeze blew and a slight chill was in the air. Inside, with all the candles lit it was too warm, outside it was a bit cool but the cool air cut down on swarming mosquitoes.

However, the girl was oblivious to all of this. Her mind was on a tall, dark, British naval officer. *Oh Gabe,* Faith thought. *In a moment of impudent pride I've ruined it. I never meant to hurt you.* Faith recalled the look of disbelief and shock on Gabe's face as she called him the enemy. Had he made his escape, she wondered.

She had made her way to Savannah as she had told Gabe she'd do. She was given sanctuary in the home of her father's friend and business partner. Gavin Lacy and his wife, Caroline, had been very kind to her. Faith had told them about her suspicions of Uncle Adam's activities, which had been rumoured for some time. It was not much later that word had made its way to Faith that Colonel Francis Marion and General Gates had gone south to Port Royal and confiscated all the supplies her uncle had stored in his warehouse. Some of Montique's men had gotten wind of the impending arrest and warned him that a warrant had been issued for treason and white slavery. Upon hearing the news from his men, Montique loaded all he could aboard one of his ships and fled just prior to General Gates's men's arrival.

One of the slaves got word to Nanny that Montique had vowed to do worse than murder to Faith and the British bastard she'd taken up with. Even with the ever-constant protection offered by Mr Lacy and his men, Faith had woken several times from a nightmare where she was being raped repeatedly while her uncle looked on laughing. Nanny had slept in her room for weeks until Faith refused for her to do so another night.

"Just look at you," Faith scolded Nanny, "Sleeping in that chair has got your lumbago so flared up you're worthless to anyone. I'll not be the cause of all your ailments flaring up. From now on you sleep in your bed."

Seeing the truth in Faith's words Nanny agreed, "You's right child, I's gonna sleep in my bed from now on wid dis heah hatchet under my pillow, and if a bad man messes wid you, chile, I's gonna chop off his head." Still before Nanny went to sleep she prayed, "Lawd, keep yo hands on the missy, dem good-fur-nuthin men of ours, and if some left over keep me in mind too, Lawd. Amen."

***

Gabe had met with his officers and caught up on what had happen during his absence.

"The ship is in good repair. We need a few things but are ready for sea now if need be," Hazard had assured Gabe.

Nathan Lavery brought up the subject of Mr Davy. "Is Mr Davy gone for good, sir?" the lieutenant asked. "If so, we have an opening for another mid."

Gabe made a note to check on this when he dined with his brother that evening. He didn't go into specifics, but before dismissing his officers, Gabe said, "I have every belief we will be putting to sea very soon to engage a fair-sized force. When I told the men, tomorrow we work, I meant it. Starting tomorrow I want the crew put through all the drills. They know sailing and gunnery, and I want them to be put through fire drill. Drill them on what to do if the tiller cable parts and we lose steerage. I want to see who steps forward if all the officers are killed."

Looking at the captain, Blake spoke what the others were thinking, "You think we're in for a substantial battle with a sizable force, don't you, sir?"

Gabe would not lie to his officers, "I have no way of knowing exactly what we're to face, Mr Blake, but I do expect the worse. If we prepare for it and there's less...well we can all be thankful."

***

The officers had gone back topside and Gabe could hear the men padding around on the deck overhead going through their daily activities. Gabe had just finished writing in his journal "crew employed A.T.S.R.," the abbreviation for as the service requires, when he heard the challenge "boat ahoy" *Le Frelon*!

That could only be Earl, Gabe thought as he grabbed his hat and headed topside. It appeared Lord Anthony had given the corvette to Earl. *It was past time he had his own ship,* Gabe thought. *In reality he should have had a command before me.* Before he left the cabin, Gabe called out, "Dawkins?"

"Aye, Cap'n."

"I'm thinking we're about to have a small celebration. Some glasses and a bit of something tasty if you will."

"Aye, Cap'n, right away."

"Lum?"

"Yes, suh…aye, sir."

"Get your lotz. I want to show it to my friend."

Looking at Dawkins, Lum replied, "Aye, aye sir." Then Lum looked pleased as Dawkins grinned and nodded his head.

"We'll make a sailor outta you yet, Lum, and that's no error."

The two seem to be getting along well, Gabe thought. Then it occurred to him that Dagan had made himself scarce of late and come to think of it so had Caleb, undoubtedly to give him time to clear his thoughts on the ordeal that he had been through…then thinking of Caleb, Gabe thought of Mr Jewels.

"Damme," Gabe said to himself, "How my mind wonders," as he climbed the companionway he couldn't help but wonder what if any mischief the ape had been up to.

***

Dagan made his way into *SeaWolf's* captain's cabin without the usual announcement by the marine sentry. He caught Gabe's eye, then holding up his watch he alerted him to the time, and then he disappeared into the pantry.

After seeing Dagan, Gabe patted his friend on the shoulder and said, "Stephen, old salt, I hate to be a bad host but its time I sup with the Admiral."

Earl then looked at his own watch, "Damme, Gabe, where has the time gone? You'd best make headway to the flagship. You can't keep the Admiral waiting even if he is your brother."

"Aye," Gabe answered. "Sometimes it's hard keeping the two separated."

The two had shared more than enough wine, biscuit, fresh preserves, and cheese in celebration of Earl's promotion to Master and Commander and being given command of *Le Frelon*. Now Gabe wondered if he'd be able to do justice to his meal at the flagship. Earl had enjoyed Lum's lotz and commented on how like a flute it was but still different in tone. "It has a melancholy sound does it not?"

"Aye," Gabe replied. "But Lum can make it dance a jig as well." The three had passed it around and made attempts at mastering the instrument with instructions from Lum. Earl seemed to grasp it more readily than Gabe whose talents seemed to be more with stringed instruments.

Surprisingly Lum did well with Gabe's lute and said he'd played a violin as well. "We have a master musician in our mist," declared Earl, which seemed to please the old black man.

Even with the distinct separation of officers and crew, Lum seemed to be treated better than he'd ever been treated as a slave. Dagan had told him, "You're a slave no more. You're a free man and will be paid for your labours. The Royal Navy don't pay well but it pays and being the Cap'n's servant you'll have more freedom than most."

As Earl waited for his gig he shook Gabe's hand. "Thank you again. Lord Anthony told me you'd thought of me when the corvette was taken." Gabe was touched by the sincerity in his friend's voice.

"Nonsense, Stephen, you were the only real candidate His Lordship had."

"Well, I hope I meet his expectations," Earl replied. "I'd hate to fail His Lordship in anyway."

"I had the same concerns," Gabe admitted. "There were some whose whispers were not so silent as not to be overheard. It was said that had I not been the son of one admiral and brother of another I'd never been given command at such an early age. A crib captain was one description I heard. Therefore, it was very important for me to succeed and my appointment not be viewed as that of special interest but be viewed as an accomplishment."

Hazard, the first lieutenant, approached the two captains in conversation and stood waiting until he was acknowledged.

"Yes, Mr Hazard?" Gabe stated.

"My compliments, sir, and Captain Earl's gig is waiting, sir."

"Thank you, Mr Hazard." As Gabe walked to the entry port with his friend, Earl grasped his arm. He stopped suddenly and faced Gabe.

"The captain's call tomorrow Gabe…is it something big, something important?" Unsure of what to say but not wanting to make Earl wonder for another several hours he replied, "I'm not sure of what the Admiral's order will be, but were it I with a new command and an unproven crew I'd spend time in gunnery drill."

Earl gave Gabe a knowing look, "Gunnery drill it will be then, sir. Gunnery drill it'll be."

***

As Gabe boarded the flagship to dine with his brother he saw Bart smoking his pipe while sitting on one of the huge twelve-pounder cannons.

"Tell me, Bart," Gabe said, "how have Silas and Mr Jewells been doing during my absence?"

Bart's face broke out in a grin, "Ah…Gabe, it's been exciting at times, it has. Silas made a platter full of pastries for 'is Lordship's breakfast and put 'em on the table. Then 'e went to fetch some coffee. When 'e returned 'is Lordship was sitting at the table and all the pastries were gone. Silas thinks 'is Lordship must've been hungry, but he pour's 'is coffee as be usual. He then goes back to 'is 'ole.

"Soon His Lordship calls, 'Silas, is there anything to break my fast?' Surprised Silas says, 'My Lord, I put a whole platter of berry pastries on the table.' 'Well, they were not here when I sat down.' 'But My Lord, they be right there when I went to fetch your coffee.' 'Well, damme, man,' His Lordship growled, 'I didn't eat the damn things and I'm hungry so find something for me directly.' 'Aye, My Lord.' Then Silas, puzzled as 'e can be, see'd me. 'Did you eat 'is Lordship's pastries, Bart?' 'Nay, I just come up from me own mess,' I swore. Now Silas is really fit to be tied but 'e busies himself fixing 'is Lordship's breakfast. No sooner 'ad 'e set it down for 'is Lordship than Mr Jewells let loose wid a fart that would make a broadside dull in comparysum. And stink— gawd, it was terrible. Pure made 'is Lordship's eyes water and 'e gagged like 'e was bout to spew.

"'Damme, sir, but that was foul,' he said to Silas, 'is Lordship thinking it was Silas what smelt up the cabin so bad. Then der was a nutter fart only Silas was at 'is Lordship's side and the fart sounded from the pantry. This un smelt worse than the first and set 'is Lordship to gagging again. Not wanting Silas to have to clean up spew from 'is Lordship, I took hold and said, 'Come with me sir, let's go topside to breathable air.' We bout knocked the sentry arsehole over teakettle as we flew from the cabin. The marine looking ill 'is own self as the smell follered us outta the cabin.

"It was just a minute or two when I seen ole Silas aft by the taffrail. He was greener than a frog at the gills. 'Silas, what's wrong wid you man?' 'It were the ape.' 'The ape?' I quizzed. 'Aye, the ape what done it. It was him that ate 'is Lordship's whole tray of pastries. He 'ad berry stains on 'is face and fingers.'

"'Ah,' I said, 'Them berries gave 'im the farts.'

"'Nay,' Silas said, 'Not farts, shats. That ape done shat all in 'is Lordship's pantry.'"

Gabe laughed till his eyes watered at Bart's story.

"Took a barrel-o-lemons squeezed on the deck two or three times a day for a week for the smell to finally go about. His Lordship promised a flogging if Silas ever brought Mr Jewells back in 'is cabin. That night the flag captain took pity on 'isLordship and gave an invitation to be 'is guest for supper.

***

Gabe was still in a humorous mood as he made his way to the great cabin. As he was announced he couldn't help but notice the table was only set for two. So this was an unofficial meeting. Brothers, not admiral and lieutenant.

"Ah, Gabe, I've missed you boy."

"I've missed you too, Gil," Gabe replied, using his brother's name. "I had times when I worried we'd not see each other again."

"I worried about that also, but trusting in God and Dagan's lady luck, I wouldn't give up on you."

Gabe could see moisture in his brother's eye and feeling it build in his eye quickly changed the tone of the meeting. "I say, Gil, while I was being held I thought I'd starve and the only thing I could think of was Silas's berry pastries. Did you and Mr Jewells eat them all or is any left?"

Gil looked blank at first, and then a smile creased his face. "That damn ape. I ought to have the damn thing set adrift. A menace he is, but now that Caleb's back, I guess he'll be your worry. Speaking of Caleb, he seems changed somehow. Not the rash, glib tongue he usually is."

"Aye," Gabe replied, "I think the man has been shot by one of cupid's arrows."

With the two brothers looking at each other Gil replied, "I understand you may have been pierced by one of those arrows yourself."

A smile touched Gabe's face and nodding his head in acknowledgement he said, "Dagan or Caleb or both have been talking too much, but I'll not deny it. An angel to look upon, but a mouth like a sailor at times. I have lost my heart," a sincere Gabe said to his brother, again feeling moisture return to his eyes.

Gil stood and walked over to where his brother sat and clapped a hand across his shoulders, "It must have been rough."

It was then it all came forth, the pent-up emotions came flooding out. Gil stood silently, hand on his brother's back supporting him and listening as Gabe described his ordeal. A silent Bart and Silas sat in the pantry. Dagan had told part of it but now the true depth of the ordeal came through.

Aye, Bart thought. *Brothers, but more like father and son.*

By the time Gabe had bared his soul, his concerns over his actions as commander in charge of the convoy, his captivity, and his lost love, he was feeling much better. A burden lifted.

Gil was careful in the wording of his thoughts on leaving the convoy in the hands of someone less experienced. However, the information obtained because of it had proved most important. They would have to wait and see how things ultimately played out.

Then the subject changed to Faith. "Do you think it could work out, Gil?" Gabe's voice almost pleaded for an affirmative.

"I don't know Gabe. I know I never loved till I met Lady Deborah. Had it not been for Lord McKean's death by those blackguards, we would have never been as one. Therefore, all I can say is if it was meant to be, it will be."

The two then dined on cod, green beans, new potatoes, and hot bread and after a light wine, coffee and berry pastries. They talked of their father and family in England.

Then as the evening was drawing near, Gabe asked, "Will you put forth a battle plan tomorrow?"

"Aye," Gil replied. "I've no doubt in the reliability of those papers; I just fear we will be spread too thin with such a few ships. I've sent a fair copy of the plans to

Admiral Lord Howe and Admiral Graves in case Admiral Howe is not reached. But, aye, I fear we have a battle before us. One that is coming from all points."

"I'll do my duty," Gabe said stoically.

"I've no doubt," Gill said, "Not as your brother or as your admiral. But be careful. You've had enough close calls already. Your mother and Lady Deborah would never forgive me if I allowed anything else to happen to you."

"Don't worry," Gabe replied. "I'll take care. I've a rendezvous with a blonde-haired beauty in the southern colonies. Say, Gil, what would my children look like with a dark handsome father and a beautiful blonde mother?"

"I don't know what they'd look like but they'd be imps every one, I'm thinking."

"Aye, imps they'd be."

"Gabe."

"Yes!"

"Happy birthday!"

"Damme, Gil, I'd forgotten, I can't believe I forgot my own birthday."

"You didn't, it's not till tomorrow."

"Tomorrow."

"Aye, tomorrow, Gabe."

Chapter Four

The next morning all the captains gathered in the admiral's stateroom. Wanting to start the meeting in such a way as to set the men at ease before delving into the task at hand, Lord Anthony had Bart pass out a paper he'd had his secretary and the flag captain's secretary copy.

Captain Moffett cleared his throat to get the captains' attention. Most had gathered in a group to congratulate Earl on his promotion and his new command.

"Gentlemen," Lord Anthony began, "We have some serious business before us today. If you will gather in little groups of three, my cox'n will hand out a fair copy of some papers Lieutenants Markham and Anthony were able to obtain when they boarded the corvette that is now under British colours and commanded by our own Commander Earl."

"Here, here," the group said in unison, to which Earl rose from his side chair and gave an exaggerated bow.

"Now, sirs, these papers are being handed out with the full knowledge that each of you, loyal as British subjects as well as naval officers are expected not only to know, but to do your duty." Lord Anthony's voice was very firm as he spoke. "Dagan, if you will pass out the papers to the groups."

Before the last two groups of men had gotten their papers, laughter was erupting from the first two groups. *Good,* thought Lord Anthony. *If they can see the humour in my joke and laugh at it they'll surely be ready to fight.*

As Bart went topside he met up with Dagan. Lighting up his pipe, Dagan asked, "What stirred the captains so?"

Bart gave Dagan a copy and soon he was chuckling as he read:

> *Advertisement in Boston newspaper recruiting crew for privateer Deane.*
>
> *An invitation to all brave Seamen and Marines, who have an inclination to serve their Country and make their Fortunes.*
>
> *The Grand Privateer ship DEANE,*
>
> *commanded by ELISHA HINMAN, Esq.; and prov'd to be a very capitol Sailor, will Sail on a Cruise against the Enemies of the United States of America, by the 20th instant. The DEANE mounts thirty Carriage Guns, and is excellently well calculated for Attacks, Defense and Pursuit—This therefore is to invite all those Jolly Fellows, who love their country, and want to make their fortunes at one Stroke, to repair immediately to the Rendezvous at the Head of His Excellency Governor Hancock's Wharf, where they will be received with a hearty Welcome by a Number of Brave Fellows there assembled, and treated with that excellent Liquor call'd GROG which is allow'd by all true Seamen, to be the LIQUOR OF LIFE.*

***

After the men had had their laugh, Lord Anthony spoke again in a very grave manner, "I do have in my possession a document that was captured by our esteemed Lieutenants as earlier mentioned. This document, unlike the one you've just read, has warned us of a grave and serious impending threat. This is the thirteenth day of November and if this document is still correct an attempt will be made by a consortium of privateers along with armed soldiers to invade and occupy Nova Scotia the nineteenth of this month."

"Gawd," growled Captain Buck, "That barely gives us time to get ready."

"Isn't that an odd time to propose an invasion?" asked Lieutenant Kerry.

"Ah, to the contrary," responded Captain Pope, "When better to attack than at a season when the weather is changing and attention is being given to the weather and not to defence." Realizing he might have spoken out of turn, Pope turned to the admiral, "Am I right, My Lord?"

"That you are, Captain Pope. Gentlemen, I should not have to remind you of the secrecy of the subject we are discussing but before I go further let me say this. Your first officers will be told." Then looking at Bush and Kerry added, "Or those serving as your second in command and no one else."

"Why the secrecy, My Lord?" Lieutenant Bush asked, "Surely preparations will have to be made that will be obvious to all."

"Aye, young sir, you are right in part," Lord Anthony answered, "We know the enemy has at least two agents here in Halifax. Tomorrow I will make it known that we as a squadron are being summoned to Philadelphia. That will justify the necessary movements required to make ready for sea. Now I will pass this document around for each of you to review, and we'll talk about a plan of defence."

He then passed the document to Captain Pope who was next in seniority to the flag captain and it was passed on down creating comments, as each man reviewed the document when it was passed to him.

Plans for the Invasion and Occupation of Nova Scotia

Knowing the great importance Nova Scotia will be to us and the relief our friends there stand in need of, I am happy to inform you of a consortium of free enterprise merchants have met and the sentiments of the general officers of said consortium have agreed to invade Nova Scotia.

I had the honour of writing you on the nineteenth of June, and then informed you of having engaged two persons in Nova Scotia on the business recommended in your letter of the tenth.

I would now beg to leave mention, that the persons sent information favorably of the expediency and practicability of the proposed measure. They advised the men necessary for the expedition can be raised from the Province of Maine.

Upon these recommendations the necessary men have been easily engaged. They are willing and ready to embark from Round Island on Machias Bay the dawn of November 19th. The determination for this date is the season is most favorable in regard to when defenses on land and at sea are mostly reduced due to weather.

The terms mentioned in their plan were for each consortium member to receive 10,000£ for their involvement in the scheme plus favorable consideration in regards to land and other purchases.

Unless otherwise notified I will assume the terms are agreeable and by the power you've invested in me detach the men and ships as previously stated.

The attack and invasion has been so planned that when executed the consortium will send men in arms aboard fully armed transports to attack several targets as recommended by those persons in Nova Scotia.

Men will be landed at Hampton, Yarmouth, Liverpool, Lunenburg, and Halifax. It is only at Halifax resistance is expected. In addition to British naval forces, there is usually a garrison of some two hundred British troops.

A diversion consisting of two ships will be made. These ships are at Sable Island and if the British admiral gives chase, this will lessen Halifax's defense. If the British does not fall for the ruse the ships will support the main attack.

The command of the leading ship has been given to Jeremiah O'Brian based on his part in the capture of the Margaretta now renamed Machia's Liberty.

After all the gathered men had read the document Lord Anthony asked, "Any comments?"

Captain Pope cleared his throat and then spoke, "A question, My Lord. There has long been concern the French may enter the war in support of the colonials. Do you see this capture of the French corvette, *Le Frelon,* and her French captain as proof of that concern?"

"Well, I'm not sure," Lord Anthony replied. "I'm sure the French have strongly encouraged these types of activities, but for now all we have is a privateer with a letter of marque."

"Rogues!" Lieutenant Kerry exclaimed.

"Rogues they may be, sir, but they've done more to interrupt our convoys and prolong the war than anyone else, even John Paul Jones himself. We'll worry about the French when and if they enter the war. However, for now let's worry about the matter at hand."

"How do we defend so many invasion sights with so few ships?" Lieutenant Bush asked, and then continued, "Even with the gunboat we captured and the corvette Gabe and Markham took, we have only nine vessels, and they will not go far in preventing an invasion if we are spread out."

Captains Pope and Buck were conferring and appeared about to speak when Gabe stood up.

"Why do we have to defend, My Lord?" All eyes turned to Gabe.

"What was that?" The flag captain Moffett asked.

"I said, sir, with all respect, why do we have to defend? I say we should attack. We know from those documents," Gabe said nodding his head at the papers laying on the table, "where they will launch the attacks from and on what date. I say we divide our forces." The other captains were very attentive now.

"Go on," Lord Anthony prodded.

"We can send a frigate or maybe a frigate and a cutter to Sable Island to deal with the ships there. Then the other frigate can sail up into the Bay of Bundy and position itself to protect Hampton. *Warrior* can be stationed at the mouth of Halifax Harbour and the rest of us can meet the privateers as they make their way out of Machia's Bay and past Gran Manan Island. They'll not be expecting us, so surprise will be on our side. The way I've figured it, My Lord, we've trumped their every move."

"It sounds good, lieutenant," Captain Moffett said, "but remember this is not whist and there's more at stake than a card game."

Buck and Earl had risen, "We think Gabe is right, My Lord," Buck volunteered.

"Very well," Lord Anthony replied, "Let's break out the charts and get a better feel for what routes they'll have to take." Then turning to Gabe, Lord Anthony asked, "Have you spoken of this to anyone?"

"Aye, sir," Gabe replied, "I discussed it with Lieutenant Markham on two occasions. Mr Davy was present for part of one conversation but he heard no specifics."

"Anyone else?" the admiral firmly asked the lieutenants.

"No, sir," Markham replied.

When Gabe hesitated, the admiral spoke again, "Lieutenant Anthony?"

"Well, sir, I did discuss it with one other."

"Who, sir?"

"Dagan, My Lord."

A relief went over Lord Anthony's face as a general sigh escaped from Buck and Pope and the other gathered captains. No one would doubt Dagan's discretion, certainly not the admiral and that was all that mattered.

***

Halifax Harbour became a beehive of activity as Lord Anthony's ships were made ready for sea. Since the word had been "rumoured" that the fleet was headed south, the ships took on stores as would be necessary for the trip. This was to add credibility to the story, when in truth, whether the battle was won or lost, the ships would only need one good day's supplies on board. Anyone spying on the harbour, however, would see what they would expect to see: water hoys plying back and forth, victuallers, ship's boats, and finally the ordnance barges.

Gabe was visiting Stephen Earl on board *Le Frelon*. It was Gabe's first visit since Earl had taken command. There was an obvious change in the ship's overall appearance. The smells of the freshly holystoned decks and fresh pitch filled the air. Cannons had been cleaned and blackened, ropes were neatly coiled. Brick dust had been taken to the brass work and now it shined brighter than it probably had since the ship was launched.

"What a farce," Earl said, speaking of all the comings and goings of smaller craft.

"Aye," Gabe replied, "But a necessary one if we're to maintain surprise."

At that time, Mr Boyd approached. He was Earl's first lieutenant and came from *Merlin*, where he had been Captain Buck's third lieutenant. "Pardon me, sir, but the twenty new hands have arrived as you mentioned. Would you care to speak to the men?"

Earl looked at Gabe who tried to hide his smile. "No, Mr Boyd, turn them over to the bosun," Earl replied, "He'll take care of them."

As the lieutenant went to do his bidding, Earl shook his head and said, "He means well and seems quite knowledgeable, but he's a long way from where I expect my first lieutenant to be."

"He'll learn quickly," Gabe said.

"Huh," snorted Earl, "he better, cause I'm thinking we're about to face an enemy like we've not done before."

"Do you think my plan is wrong?" Gabe asked his friend.

"No, Gabe. With no more at our disposal than what we have and there being no time for reinforcements, I think it's as good a plan as we could have. I do think the butcher's bill will be high whether we win or lose. Those privateers will be crowded with fighting men for the invasion. It may sound cruel but I intend to sink what I can rather than come together and be overrun by large numbers."

"I agree," Gabe said then asked, "Have you a surgeon yet?"

"Unfortunately not, and there's a possibility we won't have. By the way," Earl continued, "Rumour has it Caleb has been smitten by some little rebel girl."

Gabe felt a pang at the term *rebel girl*, as it made him think of Faith. Seeing the look come over Gabe's face, Earl realized he might have blundered.

"Forgive me, Gabe, I did not mean to be callous or insensitive."

Clapping his hand on his friend's shoulder Gabe said, "It's nothing." Then went on to explain, "Caleb has found himself infatuated with a young lady, Dagan's niece."

"Well, damme," Earl exclaimed, "I'd tread lightly if I were Caleb. I'd not want Dagan angry with me."

Chapter Five

The men were at their stations and the guns had all been made ready. The marines were ready, what few they were. The deck had been wet down and sanded. Though wetting the deck down now appeared to have been a wasted effort. A heavy fog seemed to leave all in its wake wet.

Now it was time to wait. Hurry up, move your arses, then wait. The darkness finally gave way to dawn, a foggy dawn.

"It will break by mid-morning," Blake, the master said.

"That's a long time," an anxious Gabe replied. "Is there any sign of *Swan*, *Le Frelon*, or *Pigeon*?"

"Aye, sir." Lavery said. "The *Swan* is to larboard and *Le Frelon* is to starboard. I can't see the ketch but on last sighting she was on station with *Le Frelon*."

Silence filled the deck. Every sound a ship makes at sea seems to be magnified by the silence. The fog moved across the deck and through the rigging in a ghostly eerie silence then disappeared only to be replaced by another patch, leaving moisture as its only sign of having been present. The master wiped the compass with a dry cloth, and Dagan taking Gabe's glass wiped the lens thoroughly though damn little good it would do as the next patch of fog would have it cloudy all over again.

Out of the corner of his eye, Gabe saw Lum whispering to Dagan who nodded and was now making his way to the wheel.

"Lum says he hears something not unlike the flap of the sail on the fishing yawl back home when the wind would fill the sail then die down."

"He's right," Gabe said. "I've heard the sound a time or two but couldn't make it out. Pass the word to the lookouts to watch for small boats, not just ships, Mr Hazard."

"Aye, Captain."

"I don't like the feel of the wind," the master, Blake, complained. "It's from the north but seems to bounce off yonder island. I …" There was a confused shouting to larboard, then a flash as a gun was fired.

A lookout shouted, "A gunboat, a black gunboat, sir, just let off a gun, can't tell if it hit anyone."

"Damme, sir, but it sounded like a thirty-two pounder."

"Aye, that it did, Mr Hazard."

Then she was visible again. A gunboat with one large gun mounted high on her bow. She had a lugsail and four sets of sweeps to manoeuvre her with when there was no wind. The marines were quick into action pouring round after round from their muskets and *SeaWolf's* swivel guns into the smaller boat from their places in the rigging before she disappeared into the heavy fog bank. Then a flash of light, somebody set off a flare. Was it Earl on *Le Frelon* or the privateers?

Makes no difference, Gabe thought, as in that one burst of light he saw what looked like six or more sets of sails dead ahead. Firing was sporadic and if anything was being hit it was not obvious yet. He felt suddenly queasy thinking what that thirty-two pounder would do to *Swan* if she were hit. Then a thunderous roar and flashes to starboard.

"That was Earl, I'm sure," Lavery said, his voice suddenly excited and high pitched.

"What was he firing at? Another gunboat? The ships ahead were not yet in range."

Meanwhile aboard *SeaWolf* with still no visible target, the gun crews sat at their stations, restless and uncomfortable now that the north wind was gathering in force.

"Fog will be gone quick like," the master proclaimed but that did nothing for the men as they shuffled and shivered, damp from the fog and cold from the wind. Gabe wished he hadn't ordered the galley fires out; a warm cup of coffee would have lifted their spirits if nothing else.

It was like holes in the sky as the sun was finally able to punch its way through the clouds. "Maybe we can see now, sir," the first lieutenant volunteered.

"And pray we be truly thankful for that which we are about to see," Gabe replied sarcastically but was suddenly sorry for his words. "My apologies, Mr Hazard, I'm foul company this morning I fear."

Another patch of fog rolled across the waves and with its passing the sky was almost clear. And with the clear sky the glimpse of sails Gabe had seen earlier, they were dead ahead and stretched across the horizon.

The lookout was calling down, "Six…no…seven sets of sails, sir and one's a frigate."

"What about the damn gunboats?" Gabe called.

"No sign, sir."

"We'll have to tack soon," Hazard volunteered, "The master has stated the sooner the better."

A number of smaller islands were now visible from the masthead and just beyond them a larger island, Grand Manan. Their present tack would take them dangerously close to those smaller islands.

"If it ain't the privateers, it's shoals and rocks," the master declared.

"Signal from *Le Frelon*, sir, engage enemy, single action."

"Damned cheeky of Earl if you ask me." Turning, Gabe was face to face with Caleb, "Thinks he's a commodore no doubt."

Gabe had to smile, "Come to grab a bit of fresh sea, sir, before the excitement starts?"

"Aye," Caleb replied, and then asked, "What does Earl mean single action?"

"We'll break through the enemy's lines as a group then it's every man or every ship for himself."

"Did I hear the lookout say one was a frigate?"

"That you did, my friend, but it's a small one, twenty-eight or thirty-two guns I'm sure, not a forty-four like *Drakkar*."

"Deck there, the frigate has fired but ain't yet found the range."

Caleb looked at his friend, "Have a care and no heroics today. Your word."

Grasping Caleb's hand Gabe replied, "My word."

"Liar," Caleb responded then made his way below to recheck everything he'd already checked and make sure his mates were sober.

***

"Earl will have his hands full today," Hazard volunteered. He had gotten to know the man well during his temporary command of *SeaWolf.* "A very confident seaman and brave man. May God and luck be with him this day."

"Aye," Lavery answered. He too liked Earl and was concerned about his having to face a thirty-two-gun frigate with a twenty-gun corvette.

"Not worried about the odds are you Mr Lavery?" Blake, the master asked.

"Who wouldn't be," Lavery responded matter-of-factly. "A schooner, a ketch, a brigantine, and a corvette against God knows what."

Overhearing the two lieutenants' conversation Gabe didn't speak out but felt the same apprehension. It had sounded like the best plan available back in *Warrior's* wardroom…but now. Well now, the plan was in effect and that was all there was to it.

"Shall I go aloft?" Dagan asked. He knew Gabe needed him at the masthead but seemed reluctant to order it.

"Yes, let me know what we are facing, a true picture."

The lookout moved over as Dagan made his way onto the platform. A quick scan of three hundred sixty degrees then Dagan settled his attention to the sails ahead. After scanning the horizon again, Dagan called down his report.

"Seven ships and a gunboat, a galley I believe and there's wreckage aft, probably the gunboat we saw earlier."

Probably a forward scout, Gabe thought.

As quickly as he'd gone aloft Dagan was quicker coming back down and expanding on his report. "Seven ships and a large galley. Looks like three large schooners, sixteen or eighteen guns I'm thinking, a brig at least sixteen guns and the frigate. There's one ship aft I couldn't get a good look at and the galley appears to have a thirty-two pounder forward."

As the ships continued to approach on a converging tack Hazard approached Gabe, "It appears *Le Frelon* will be on one quarter and we'll be on the other of that frigate."

"Aye," Gabe answered, "If we can time it right we can both give her a broadside and hopefully she'll not have enough gunners to deliver a full blow from both sides at once. However, don't forget, sir, we have a large schooner to our larboard that will be doing her damnedest to cripple us as well."

"Aye, sir, I see her more clearly now."

"Deck there, the schooner has just fired a bow chaser in our direction."

It was a wet sailing master who turned inboard and growled. "A miss, but close enough to soak me, by gawd. He'll have our range with the next one, I'm thinking."

Hearing the master's comments, Gabe spoke to his lieutenants, "To your stations now. Keep a good lookout, and after my first order to fire, fire as you will.

Remember it will be close action and from all quarters so don't wait for me to tell you what to do…just do it."

As the two left Gabe looked over toward *Swan*. He could make out Markham and Davy. Both gave a wave and Gabe returned it.

"We'll all share a wet when this is over," Dagan spoke softly.

"I'm looking forward to it." Then Gabe made his way to the wheel. "All ready, Mr Blake?"

"Aye, Cap'n, we're ready by gawd."

Then speaking to the crew in general, Gabe called out, "A guinea to every member of the gun crew whose gun scores the first hit." This set the men to howling. "Mind you…mind you now. Men!" Gabe spoke again after quieting the men, "If there's a tie you'll have to share the purse but I'll double the rum ration."

This again set the men to howling. This was what he wanted…to get the men in the right mood for what was forthcoming.

***

BOOM!…CRASH!…

The master was right. The approaching ships now had their range, and it would be a minute more before their guns would be in range; however, Earl had just let loose with a forward gun.

"Alter our course two points to windward," Gabe ordered the helmsman, "Then let's see if yon frigate notices the change before she fires again."

BOOM!…BOOM!…The frigate fired at Earl who quickly returned fire.

"A hit, a hit. *Le Frelon* has scored a hit."

"The hornet has stung its prey," Dagan quipped.

"Let's hope he does more than just sting him," Blake replied after hearing Dagan's comment.

The converging schooner let off a gun. The shot landed close to *SeaWolf's* bowsprit sending a spout of water over the bow and soaking a gun crew. Still Gabe held his fire.

"Alter course again back to original course," Gabe ordered the helmsman. "No use wasting shots yet," Gabe spoke his thoughts aloud.

But the frigate was not concerned about range and fired another bow chaser at *LeFrelon.*

"She's hit, *Le Frelon* has been hit," called down the lookout but Gabe could see with his own eyes.

The bowsprit was broken and dragging in the water. You could hear the officer's shouts and soon the bosun and a group of men with axes were chopping away at the wreckage and soon cast it adrift.

More gunfire, more flashes as Gabe made his way forward to get a better view. There was something unreal about all that was taking place. It was dreamlike. Then they were upon the privateers. A sudden exploding sound, a stupendous roar that could only be a broadside from the frigate filled the air. Loud whooshing, howling sounds were heard as the air was rent by flying cannon balls, half the wheel and the gaff boom were shattered with splinters flying everywhere.

Fire, had he given the order to fire? "Fire," he shouted, "Fire at will."

Great pieces of the bulwark were missing, a huge gouge in the deck, guns upturned, the rigging falling. Looking up at the sails Gabe saw holes open up as shot after shot passed through them.

Then where there had been booms, *probably twelve pounders,* Gabe thought, there were now pops from the schooner, puppies yapping when compared to the frigate's thunder.

The frigate was now on the starboard beam and the large rebel schooner to larboard. *SeaWolf* was being fired on from both quarters. Balls whizzed overhead, tearing at the upper rigging while other balls were finding their mark as they tore into the ship's hull.

CRASH!…loud screams filled the air as another of the frigate's ball found its mark. The ball had overturned another of *SeaWolf's* forward guns, crushing several of the gun crew. Gabe felt dazed as the air felt like it was sucked from his chest as a ball flew past. Watching it cross the deck, it appeared to be moving in slow motion until it hit one of the marines. Suddenly the man was without his legs. He fell to the deck, his lower body a gory pulp. Another crash…a group of men were cut down with the ball leaving a bloody path across the decking before the ball bounced up taking out a stanchion. As the frigate and the schooner continued their onslaught on *SeaWolf,* Gabe felt a great shudder as if she was trying to shake off the attack from her foes. *Damme,* he thought. *My ship is getting chopped to pieces.*

Men were down, bleeding, reaching out for help. Some were crying while others were screaming and writhing in pain from their injuries. Others mercifully lay silent, staring at the sky through sightless eyes.

The ship was completely engulfed in smoke. From aloft the enemy fire was making its mark as riggings separated then flew apart. Blocks and tackles plunged to the deck, some hitting harmlessly while others crashed into unsuspecting sailors with a sickening thud. That was it, knowing that ship-to-ship they were no match for *SeaWolf*, the schooners were trying to cripple the brigantine by bringing down her riggings. The smoke began to clear as the wind carried it away. *To leeward, they were closing with the islands, too damn close*, Gabe thought. Then a bellowing roar as several of the larboard guns let loose; a roar that shook the deck beneath his feet.

"That's it boys give them another round," Lavery called out. A cheer came from the gun crews, the schooner had been hit hard…so hard she was dead in the water. The marine's sharpshooters continued to fire at human targets. Then they were past the enemy and in the clear.

Without hesitating, Gabe called out, "Prepare to go about."

Dagan appeared at his side, "Mr Hazard has been hit, sir, hit hard. He may lose his arm if not more."

"Is he below yet?" Gabe asked.

"Aye, just after we passed through the line."

"Very well. Mr Lavery!"

"Aye, Cap'n"

"You have the deck. Have the ship put about."

"Aye, aye, Cap'n."

"Dagan, you will take Mr Hazard's place with the starboard section." Dagan nodded and Gabe went below.

Caleb already had the arm removed by the time he got there. Seeing Gabe, Caleb shook his head, "He's unconscious, and maybe he'll stay that way for a while. I took his left arm off without complications but he has a splinter in his thorax that I can't remove. He needs to be on land to have his chest cut open. Even then there's no guarantee. It might be better if he died now…without suffering."

Nodding his understanding, Gabe turned to leave then paused, "Keep him comfortable, Caleb. Losing him will be a loss I can ill afford."

***

Back on deck Gabe was surprised at the powder and smoke smudged faces of his crew. They had come about and were now overtaking a couple of the privateers. The one privateer *SeaWolf's* gunners had fired on was down in the stern and he could see several boats in the water around the sinking ship.

Swan had just come about and though she was scarred she seemed to be sailing well as was the *Pigeon*. Earl had been faster and had already come about and now was dead ahead off the larboard bow.

"Deck there! The frigate has come about and so has the largest of the schooners, sir. So 'as the brig, sir. Now the second schooner 'as come about as well."

"A final meeting!"

"Sir?"

Again Gabe had spoken his thoughts aloud without realizing it. "I said one final meeting, Mr Lavery. At least I hope we succeed with this round."

"Aye, Cap'n, I hope so as well. Ah…how was Mr Hazard, sir?"

"He's alive…the surgeon says it will be touch and go…"

"Kind of like the fix we're about to be in, isn't it Cap'n, touch and go."

BOOM!…BOOM!…

"There goes the frigate and Captain Earl again."

"Right you are, Mr Lavery, now back to your station."

"Aye, aye, Cap'n."

"Mr Blake."

"I'm sorry, sir," a master's mate replied, "I'm afraid he's done for!

"Done for? When?" a shocked Gabe inquired.

"When the frigate let loose, sir."

Damme, Gabe thought. *I didn't even realize it.* Then turning to Evans, the master's mate, he ordered, "You have control of the wheel. Follow my orders."

"Aye, sir."

I must speak with the bosun and carpenter, Gabe thought, *I fear I may not have time directly.*

***

"Mostly its betwixed wind and water, sir, more in the riggings and the upper decks," Dover, the carpenter reported. "No more water in the well than usual."

Then Graf reported, "Dagan got a party together and we's got two of the guns back into their carriages so they be back ready for action."

"Are they stable enough?" Gabe asked.

"Aye, Cap'n, jus like a newborn in 'is modder's cradle." There was another swooshing sound overhead as the enemy renewed their assault.

"Very well men, let's be about it," Gabe said dismissing the bosun and the carpenter. Glancing over, Gabe saw Lum. He seemed to be taking it all in, and then Gabe realized his breeches were smeared with gunpowder stains, as was his face and hands. Only it wasn't as noticeable due to Lum's black colour. He had been involved in fighting the ship and I didn't even notice Gabe thought. Then he wondered what Faith would say if she could see him now.

As the *SeaWolf* continued to approach the enemy schooner the lookout called down, "The frigate and the brig be 'tacking, Cap'n Earl, sir."

"*Damn*," Gabe thought. He looked and *Swan* had her own troubles. At least, *Pigeon* was almost up with her and could help. "Evans, prepare to put your helm down when I order. Dagan! I want every gun loaded, with double shot."

"Aye," Dagan replied.

"Mr Lavery, I want your section loaded with ball and canister."

"Aye, Cap'n."

As the two ships converged, Gabe looked up. The wind was holding…this never predictable and always perverse wind was holding. *Dagan's lady luck*, Gabe thought as subconsciously his hand went to the pouch around his neck. The now empty pouch. *"Please God…be with her,"* Gabe prayed silently then turned his attention back to the battle.

Looking forward, Gabe scratched his jaw and eyed the oncoming schooner. If he timed it right one by one every gun on the larboard side would get a chance to bloody her nose. If he mistimed it the schooner would ram them. Looking aloft the commission pennant's tail stood out like it was pointing the way.

"Now, Evans. Put your helm down now!"

It took a moment for the rudder to bit and that moment seemed forever before *SeaWolf* responded.

Now instead of passing side by side, they were crossing the bow of the schooner.

"As you bear Mr Lavery, fire as you bear. Rake her good."

Gun after gun gave a bellowing roar. White smoke engulfed the ship and Gabe was temporarily blinded. However, the smoke was quickly swept away. It was sickening to see what was left of the once proud schooner.

"Up helm, up helm, Evans. Dagan, be ready."

"No need, sir," this from Lavery. As Gabe looked up he saw the reason for Lavery's comment.

The schooner was on fire; flames were now shooting up her sails. People were diving into the frigid waters. Every captain's nightmare, a fire at sea.

"Dagan, see if any of the boats are still in tow and set them adrift as we pass."

"You're not going to heave to?" Evans asked.

Pointing forward with his sword, Gabe asked, "Would you have me leave Captain Earl without assistance while we pick up enemy survivors?"

"Nay, Cap'n, my apologies, my mind was adrift with the sight before me, I'm afraid."

***

"Mr Druett," Gabe called his gunner.

"Aye, Cap'n."

"Do you think your aim is good enough to hit yonder brig and not *Le Frelon?*"

"Aye, Cap'n, when in range I can knock a flea off a cat's arse without singeing 'is 'airs if ye'd like for me to."

"Nothing so precise Mr Druett, I just want to lay a few rounds about her deck."

"Aye, Cap'n. Bout 'er deck it'll be."

Any moment now, Gabe was thinking when the forward gun fired. He quickly stood on the bulwark to see if he could tell where the ball landed. He was not quick enough to see the exact spot but he did see shattered planking flying into the air.

Druett was true to his word, and then the gun fired again. This time there was no need to guess, the jubilant gun crew was jumping up and down cheering, their teeth appearing unusually white in powder-blackened faces.

"Easy lads, easy now, let's give them another with the cap'n's compliments."

"Another hit by gawd," Evans swore! "Damme, if Druett don't know his business, sir."

"Look sir," someone forward called. Through the smoke Gabe could see the brig's mast was leaning dangerously.

"Surprised we haven't been fired on." Dagan said as he made his way to Gabe.

"I'm sure they used all the crew to board *Le Frelon*. I just hope we're not too late to help Earl. Alter course, Evans, bring us along side the brig. Mr Graf, let's take in another sail."

Suddenly there was a puff of smoke from the brig and Gabe felt *SeaWolf* shudder. That had been a hard hit. He was about to call out to Druett when one of the forward guns fired, followed quickly by the other. The gunner had loaded both guns and after firing one, sighted and fired the second.

Another cheer from the gun crew let Gabe know they'd hit Druett's target. The ships were close now and Gabe was worried he'd waited to late to take in the sails.

"Dagan, Mr Lavery, prepare boarding parties. Dagan, you forward, Mr Lavery."

"Aye, Cap'n, we'll be aft."

"Mr Graf, gather the rest of the men and we'll board amidships."

"Aye, Cap'n," the bosun replied as he hurried to round up his party.

All too quick they were along side the brig. *I should have ordered the sails taken in sooner,* Gabe thought. *SeaWolf* slammed into the brig with such a jar that it shook the deck planks. The two hulls thudded together and then seemed to bounce off each other before *SeaWolf* ground to a stop. Graf's men were ready with grapnels and they were already flying through the air.

"Boarders, boarders away," Gabe called as he gained his balance. The cry was repeated forward and aft as Dagan and Lavery made their way over to the brig. The privateer's crew fired at *SeaWolf's* boarders. Musket and pistols shots rang out and balls smacked into the deck as men fell. *SeaWolf* had left a few marine sharpshooters in the rigging and they were returning fire, cutting down all they could.

A swivel gun fired defiantly, another of *SeaWolf's* marines cutting down a group of would be resistance. The boarders pushed forward, bent on reaching *Le Frelon* and helping their mates. Curses filled the air with the clang and rasp of steel upon steel.

Bellowing his loudest, Gabe directed his men to a group of four men with muskets that had gathered around the stump of the brig's mainmast. One of the sharpshooters sagged as Lum threw a boarding pike like a spear, impaling the man who fell forward his musket clanging on the deck and going off harmlessly. Another jerked convulsively as the bosun not to be outdone by Lum had hurled his boarding axe into the skull of his foe. Gabe was now upon his man. Apparently the man had already fired his musket, although Gabe couldn't recall. Maybe it had been a misfire.

At any rate the man was trying to fiend off Gabe's sword with his musket barrel. Feeling the urgency to reach Earl, Gabe made a feint that the man overreacted to; Gabe stepped inside the man's guard and brought the hilt of his sword down on the man's exposed head, felling him like an ox. Another man was racing toward Gabe when a shot rang out. Gabe heard a penetrating thump and the man's chest turned crimson as he fell to the deck.

SeaWolf's crew was making their way onto *LeFrelon* and not a moment to soon. Bodies were all over the deck, some lifeless, others wounded, bleeding and groaning. A horrible scream broke Gabe's revive. There was something unreal about the scream as it rang out above the den of battle then a falling object from above crashed onto the deck with a crunching sound. It was an enemy sharpshooter. He lay in odd angles, twisted in a heap and blood gushing from his ears and nose. One eye socket was empty. Gabe's group was rushing forward; resistance now was only in little pockets. Earl's men had put up a fearsome fight but were in danger of being overrun.

Gabe saw Lavery and his group engaged with a band of privateers. The constant sound of curses and cries were mingled with the clang of metal on metal as blades flashed in the air then clashed together. The sounds of gunshots some muffled as a pistol was shoved against a foe as the trigger was pulled. The air was heavy with the smell of gunpowder mixed with the distinct odour of death.

Out of the corner of his eye, Gabe realized Dagan was being overwhelmed by two men. As he gave ground he slipped and fell. As one of the men lunged at Dagan with his cutlass Gabe shot him with his pistol. At seeing his friend downed, the other man turned facing Gabe. The man's face twisted in rage as he rushed at the man who shot his friend. Gabe met the man's rush head-on and his sword clanged with the other's cutlass.

Then the man spat tobacco juice into Gabe's face. Some of it went into his eyes and caused his vision to blur, his eyes stung as if on fire. Gabe's opponent thought he'd won; a smile appeared on his face as he raised his cutlass to finish off Gabe. However, the man had forgotten about Dagan who had quickly regained his footing. The man's smile suddenly changed as his arm was severed from Dagan's crashing blow with his cutlass. Then Dagan whirled and drove the cutlass through the man's chest. Gabe had wiped his eyes with his coat sleeve and vision was returning as he gathered his wits.

"Earl! Stephen Earl!" Gabe called. "Earl!" His calling seemed to attract the attention of a group still fighting. The sight of the British sailors appearing unexpectedly had the privateers throwing down their weapons and raising their hands. Then it was over.

Dagan walked up to Gabe clapping him on the shoulder. "Any sign of Mr Earl?"

"Not yet."

Seeing Lavery approaching, Gabe called, "Take a party and take possession of the brig."

"Aye, Cap'n. Mr Graf, lend a hand with your party if you please."

"Aye, sir. You heard Mr Lavery, lads. Let's be quick about it now, move it. They's dead, them buggers, they ain't gonna bother you none, but careful where you step at. Blood's still wet and slick like."

"Sir...sir!" It was one of the bosun mates.

"Yes," Gabe answered.

"We've found Mr Earl, sir, he and a group of men are on board the frigate. He's trying to prevent their escape but 'ands are cutting grapnel lines."

Gabe again felt a sense of urgency, "Lieutenant Baugean!"

"Aye, sir."

"Have your marines board the frigate aft if you please."

"Aye, sir."

"Mr Baugean!"

"Sir."

"Put a couple of sharpshooters in the brig's riggings and have them mark down anyone not on our side who approaches the frigate's quarterdeck."

"Aye, Cap'n."

Then Gabe called to Dagan, "See if we can't find a few more grapnels to lash the ships together then meet me on board that frigate." Without waiting for Dagan to answer, Gabe gathered his men about him and boarded the frigate.

The frigate being a taller ship meant the men had to make their way up to her decks. This meant they were vulnerable to musket fire, exposed as they were. The sudden sound of gunfire filled the air and made Gabe pause to look, but none of his boarders appeared to have been hit, then a quick glance behind him told him it was Sergeant Schniedermirer firing onto the frigate. Then Gabe's men were on board joining the melee.

Earl's men were mostly gathered around the mainmast and most of their resistance seemed to be from the direction of the quarterdeck. "Set Fire!" A sudden volley of musket fire struck down a number of the privateers.

"Second rank fire." Lieutenant Baugean had divided his marines into two groups. The second volley caused the resistance to realize they were surrounded, and then a sailor threw down his cutlass and raised his hands in surrender. Seeing the action of their comrade the rest of the men threw down their weapons as a group.

"Where's your officer?" a bruised and bleeding Earl demanded. When no one spoke, Earl grabbed the man nearest him and with his pistol levelled it at the man's face and said, "Well?"

The poor man stood there tongue-tied, to afraid to speak. From within the group a voice, "I think they're all dead, sir."

"Who are you?" Earl demanded.

"Lawson, sir, master's mate."

"They damn well better be," Earl responded with clenched teeth. His arm dropping suddenly, Gabe and Dagan took a step forward to support him.

"I'm fine," Earl spoke, "son of a bitch showed a white flag, then as we were boarding fired on us with a swivel gun. I'd be dead but Mr Boyd was in front of me and he took most of the load. Poor man was screaming in agony. He's done for I'm sure."

At that moment a hail...Markham was there with *Swan* and so was Kerry with the ketch. Caleb, who had been sent for, was now coming over to check on Earl. As order was being restored, the death and destruction were overwhelming. Bodies were strewn so you had to step over them to get across the ship.

"Have you ever seen such a butcher's bill?" Earl asked his friend.

"Nay," replied Gabe, "But better them than us."

Epilogue

Lieutenant Kerry was sent in the ketch *Pigeon* to inform Captain Buck on *Merlin* and Lieutenant Bush on the cutter *Audacity* that the invasion had been repulsed. *Le Frelon, SeaWolf,* and *Swan* headed back to Halifax with the frigate and the brig as prizes.

Warrior was anchored at the mouth of the harbour and *Drakkar* was just beyond. Both ships situated so that their guns protected the entry into the harbour from either a northern or southern approach.

All eyes were on the approaching ships. Bart had been among the first to spot them, so he had hurried down to the admiral's quarters. Lord Anthony felt a burden lift from his shoulders as a grinning Bart approached his desk.

"Well, spit it out man," Lord Anthony said to Bart, who had a smug grin on his face. "Don't just stand there like the cat that ate the canary."

"Well," Bart said. "Reckon 'ow much money do the admiralty got?"

"How much money?" Lord Anthony responded not believing his ears or understanding Bart's question, "Why I guess they've enough, but why should that matter?"

"Cause it 'pears Gabe know'd what 'e was talking about. Here they comes and hit looks like they done got themselves a big ole frigate and a fat brig as prizes."

"Damme," Lord Anthony responded as he quickly rose, grabbed his coat and headed topside. Seeing the admiral come on deck Moffett strode over to where he was and offered Lord Anthony his glass.

"A beautiful sight, is it not, My Lord?"

"Ah...but that it is, Dutch, that it is. Have the captains repair on board as soon as convenient and send the surgeon and his mates across. I've a feeling they'll be needed."

"Aye, My Lord."

Captain Moffett greeted the three captains on deck of the flagship while reports were sent below for the admiral. After his congratulations Bart led them on down to the great cabin. As they entered the cabin the first thing that came to Lord Anthony's mind was, *They look older.*

War turns boys into men and men into old men before their time, he thought.

Anthony then noticed not only the strained looks on his officer's faces but their wounds were showing in the stiffness of their moves. Earl's shoulder seemed to be causing him considerable pain.

"It's good to see you all in one piece," Lord Anthony spoke trying to lighten the situation, then turning to Earl asked, "Do you need the surgeon?"

"No, My Lord, Caleb has done a good job. He relates I'll be stiff for awhile but should mend completely," he grimaced.

"Be seated while Silas provides a glass of wine. I think we could all do with a glass after what has transpired over the last few days," said Lord Anthony. "I'm sorry it took such a sacrifice but we can't afford to lose Nova Scotia, if we do I fear the war is lost before it begins. I know it's hard to see the worth when we lose such good men as Mr Boyd, Mr Blake, and others. I hear it's touch and go for Hazard. We'll hope and pray for the best.

"From your reports," Lord Anthony continued, "One gunboat was sunk, three schooners sunk, one schooner turned her heels after a battering engagement. A frigate and a brig were taken prize. Both appear to be seaworthy. I think their Lordships at the Admiralty will consider it a bargain, especially when we lost no ships even though you say *Le Frelon* is in a bad way."

Thinking aloud, Gabe spoke, "But what about the men? Not just ours but theirs. I will not soon forget the cries from the men in the water as I passed them."

Lord Anthony took a breath, then gave a sigh, "What would have happened to Earl and his men had you not?" he answered.

A silence engulfed the men as Silas served the wine, each thinking of those lost in battle. When Silas finished and drew back Earl asked, "We saw *Drakkar* anchored, My Lord, what happened at Sable Island?"

"Not much actually. Two privateers made a feint but seeing Drakkar and the gunboat before them, turned heels and sailed away without so much as firing a shot."

"Prudent, I would say," Markham responded.

"I guess the *Willing Maid* was not so willing," Lord Anthony joked.

"What was that?" Gabe asked. "What was the name of the ship?"

"It was the *Willing Maid.* Do you know of her?"

"Aye, My Lord, she is commanded by Malachi Mundy, a seemingly capable man. It was to him and

Jack Cunningham's *Norfolk Gold* that we transferred the women captives we released from Montique's jail."

"Oh yes, I remember now," Lord Anthony replied. "Well maybe prudent is a good description."

Suddenly, there was a knock on the door and the marine sentry announced, "Flag captain, suh."

As Moffett entered the cabin he announced, "Dispatch ship making its way to anchor, My Lord."

"Very well, gentlemen, lets go about setting your ships to rights. Unless this dispatch ship brings word to change things I'd enjoy the company of each of you for dinner tonight. As I recall two of you have just had a birthday which will add to the cause for celebration."

***

After the lieutenant from the dispatch vessel had left Bart brought a cup of Silas's special coffee to His Lordship.

"Something to warm yer bones on a frigid night, sir."

"Aye, thank you, Bart. It's most welcome and not a moment to soon."

Seeing the papers on the admiral's desk before him, Bart asked, "New orders?"

"Aye, Bart. Lord Howe is of the opinion that Nova Scotia is no longer an objective of the colonials. They've failed to secure Quebec by the army and they've now failed Nova Scotia by sea—even though he doesn't know of the failed invasion as of yet. His Lordship feels our forces are needed south. As soon as convenient we are to sail south to Philadelphia were His Lordship's words. There I'm to report to Admiral Graves for further orders."

"Well, 'I's don't mind going south," Bart volunteered, "But I wishes it'd be a bit further south. It's still cold in Fillydelfia ain't it?"

"Aye, Bart, that it is, and with December coming on I fear we will be iced in some cold harbour for months with nothing to do but try to keep from freezing."

"Well, could be you mighten talk Admiral Graves inta sending us uns to Florida to keep an eye on them dagos. We knows they's helping the privateers."

"Well, Bart, I'll pass your concerns on to the admiral and see how he responds."

"He'd respond in the right way iffen he 'ad a brain," Bart replied.

"Bart!"

"Aye, I knows I'm talking bout a King's officer." Then Bart was out the door.

"Damme," Lord Anthony exclaimed, "Will I ever get the last word in?"

A smiling Silas sat in the pantry and said to himself, "I doubt it."

Notes

[1] The name **brigantine** comes from the fact that these ships were the favorite vessels of sea brigands (pirates).

The brigantine was the second most popular type of ship built in the American colonies before 1775. (The most popular ship type was a sloop.)

A brigantine is swifter and more easily manoeuvred than larger ships, and therefore it was employed for purposes of piracy, espionage, and reconnoitering, and as an attendant upon larger ships for protection and supply or landing purposes. In the earlier days the brigantine was a vessel with two masts, square-rigged like a ship's fore-and-aft sail with a gaff and boom.

Little was required to convert a brigantine from use as a merchant ship to use as a privateer or vice versa.

[2] Excerpted from orders to an escort captain during the American Revolutionary War.

[3] Captain Jack Cunningham's character is from C.D. White's, *The Broken Sword*.

Glossary

aft. Toward the stern (rear) of the ship.

ahead. In a forward direction.

aloft. Above the deck of the ship.

bosun. Also boatswain, a crew member responsible for keeping the hull, rigging and sails in repair.

bowsprit. A large piece of timber that stands out from the bow of a ship.

brig. A two masted vessel, square rigged on both masts.

bulwarks. The sides of a ship above the upper deck.

burgoo. Mixture of coarse oatmeal and water, porridge.

canister. Musket ball size iron shot encased in a cylindrical metal cast. When fired from a cannon, the case breaks apart releasing the enclosed shot (not unlike firing buckshot from a shotgun shell.)

cat-o'-nine-tails. A whip made from knotted ropes, used to punish crewmen. Used for flogging.

chase. A ship being pursued.

coxswain. (cox'n) The person in charge of the captain's personal boat.

cutter. A sailboat with one mast and a mainsail and two headsails.

dogwatch. The watches from four to six, and from six to eight, in the evening.

fathom. Unit of measurement equal to six feet.

flotsam. Debris floating on the water surface.

founder. Used to described a ship that is having difficulty remaining afloat.

frigate. A fast three masted fully rigged ship carrying anywhere from twenty to forty-eight guns.

full and by. A nautical term meaning proceed under full sail

furl. To lower a sail.

gaff. A spar or pole extending diagonally upward from the after side of a mast and supporting a fore-and-aft sail.

galley. The kitchen area of a ship.

grog. British naval seaman received a portion of liquor every day. In 1740, Admiral Edward Vernon ordered the rum to be diluted with water. Vernon's nickname was Old Grogram, and the beverage was given the name grog in their disdain for Vernon.

halyard. A line used to hoist a sail or spar. The tightness of the halyard can affect sail shape.

handsomely. Slowly, gradually.

hard tack. Ship's biscuit.

haul. Pulling on a line.

heave to. Arranging the sails in such a manner as to stop the forward motion of the ship.

heel. The tilt of a ship/boat to one side.

helm. The wheel of a ship or the tiller of a boat.

holystone. A block of sandstone used to scour the wooden decks of a ship.

idler. The name of those members of a ship's crew that did not stand night watch because of their work, for example cooks and carpenters.

jetty. A manmade structure projecting from the shore.

jib. A triangular sail attached to the head stay.

John Company. Nickname for the Honourable East India Company.

Jonathan. British nickname for an American.

keel. A flat surface (fin) built into the bottom of the ship to reduce the leeway caused by the wind pushing against the side of the ship.

ketch. A sailboat with two masts. The shorter mizzenmast is aft of the main, but forward of the rudder post.

knot. One knot equals one nautical mile per hour. This rate is equivalent to approximately 1.15 statute miles per hour.

larboard. The left side of a ship or boat.

lee. The direction toward which the wind is blowing. The direction sheltered from the wind.

letter of marque. A commission issued by a government authorizing seizure of enemy property.

luff. The order to the steersman to put the helm towards the lee side of the ship, in order to sail nearer to the wind.

mainmast. The tallest (possibly only) mast on a ship.

mast. Any vertical pole on the ship that sails are attached to.

mizzenmast. A smaller aft mast.

moor. To attach a ship to a mooring, dock, post, anchor.

nautical mile. One minute of latitude, approximately 6076 feet—about 1/8 longer than the statute mile of 5280 feet.

pitch. (1) A fore-and-aft rocking motion of a boat. (2) A material used to seal cracks in wooden planks.

privateer. A privateer is a captain with a letter of marque that allows a captain to plunder any ship of a given enemy nation. A privateer was *supposed* to be above being tried for piracy.

prize. An enemy vessel captured at sea by a warship or privateer. Technically these ships belonged to the crown, but after review by the Admiralty court and condemnation, they were sold and the prize money shared.

powder monkey. Young boy (usually) who carried cartridges of gunpowder from the filling room up to the guns during battle.

quarterdeck. A term applied to the after part of the upper deck. The area is generally reserved for officers.

rake. A measurement of the top of the mast's tilt toward the bow or stern.

reef. To reduce the area of sail. This helps prevent too much sail from being in use when the wind gets stronger (a storm or gale).

roll. A side-to-side motion of the ship, usually caused by waves.

schooner. A North American (colonial) vessel with two masts the same size.

scuppers. Drain holes on deck, in the toe rail, or in bulwarks.

sextant. A navigational instrument used to determine the vertical position of an object such as the sun, moon, or stars.

shoal. Shallow, not deep.

skiff. A small boat.

skylark. To frolic or play, especially up in the rigging.

spar. Any lumber/pole used in rigging sails on a ship.

starboard. The right side of a ship or boat.

stern. The aft part of a boat or ship.

tack. To turn a ship about from one tack to another, by bringing her head to the wind.

taffrail. The upper part of the ship's stern, usually ornament with carved work or bolding.

transom. The stern cross-section/panel forming the after end of a ship's hull.

veer. A shifting of the wind direction.

waister. Landsman or unskilled seaman who worked in the waist of the ship.

weigh. To raise, as in to weigh anchor.

windward. The side or direction from which the wind is blowing.

yard. A spar attached to the mast and used to hoist sails.

yardarm. The end of a yard.

yawl. A two-masted sailboat/fishing boat with the shorter mizzenmast placed aft of the rudder post. Similar to a ketch.

zephyr. A gentle breeze. The west wind.

Printed in the United States
142336LV00002B/4/P